YESTERDAY AND TODAY

William Cheek

Lonely Song Publishing

YESTERDAY AND TODAY

ISBN # 978-0-615-32208-7

Cover Art and Design by Aluska Bissaro
Doll Head Reference Photograph Courtesy M. Fitzpatrick Murphy
Book Design by Aluska Bissaro

Published by:

LꞞ
Lonely Song Publishing
www.lonelysong.com

For the lonely

YESTERDAY AND TODAY

Does the past ride on the breeze that trickles under bright blue skies
Or on the deep black mountainside, or on the snowy field?
And does it ride the ocean's tide – the ocean once you looked upon
With innocence, with unharmed eyes, with spirit yet to wield
And does the past your spirit freeze, your heart forever seal...

Now...cold is the metal of the crumbling stair and black is the night. Hard is the road ahead and green the road behind. Green like the fields in spring and green like...sickness?

Sickness...or something else...envy?...no, sounds wrong...oh! Fields is in there twice...how about...no...

Enough! Give it up already. You've got nothing. Not now, not here...leave the poetry to the poets, the songs to the singers; play your strengths: think things out your own way, go deep, take out the sentiment, find the truth. Use your strengths.

Strength...

Oh, but the disease of memory! The stabbing of its reliving and the ache and melancholy as it fades...fading out, flaming out like me. Take me back! Take me back... what have I done, how have I come this way? What hap-

1

pened to the wonder? What happened to the morning dew and the dreaming fog; leaning, on the edge of comfortable sleep, against the window in the back seat as the heavy gray dawn slides all around; living for the wonder of things new – the field at sunrise, the bay at noon, the beach at night...

Stop it. Just stop...put it to rest, you...used up, absentminded...idiot! Life is here. You are here. Forget what cannot be changed. Move on.

Thus restraining his thoughts, the young man looked up. The city street was cool, channeling softly the hazy red-orange glow of a rising sun. Everything was fresh, as fresh and lifelike as the city would allow, and the man was pleasantly surprised (for he had not before traveled the sidewalk at this early hour) by the sharp impression of cleanliness brought on by swept walks and potted plants, colorful awnings over empty entryways, the coolness of the dew. The finest of all hours, he mused. Safe, clean, and almost – almost pretty.

And quiet. In an hour Broad Street would be full of cars, the city would hum, the haze would be scattered, and contemplation could cease. Only the task ahead.

Of course, the task ahead had never been so...

He broke off again, interrupted by the noise of a lone vehicle speeding loudly up from behind. He instinctively took a step to his right, away from the curb.

How long till rush hour…

And this is what happened: up ahead, maybe thirty feet, a young woman stepped – skipped, really – from an alleyway. It was bizarre: not the clothes, not the movements, not even the wild spontaneity (morning after in the city, after all…), but in the whole of the scene he clearly perceived some indefinable strangeness.

Only one word worked: *twirling*. Ten to seven in the morning and this girl was *twirling*, performing some ridiculous drunken happy dance directly in his path. Well. He slowed his step and cast his eyes down to her feet, refusing to offer any gaze, any invitation. No invitations, not to early morning twirlers.

She was wearing heels, but she danced lightly on her toes. For a few steps, at least. It could not have been more than just few steps, a few seconds of silly, meaningless lighthearted movement. Only the aura of incredible excitement in her motions (again, the bizarreness of it all…) somehow created a sensation of greater significance. That was all, so he thought later.

Regardless, the dance came quickly to an end. With a leap and one final twirl she landed delicately on her toes before planting her high heels emphatically into the pavement. One heel did not stop.

It was an old story, the sidewalks of the city. The papers would not let it rest: dangerous crevasses, hazardous pedestrian potholes…one must be careful when stomping around, especially in the uneven drive of an alleyway. What could she have been thinking, he thought amusedly (knowing full well that a person in such a condition as hers would not bother with foot placement, nor be bothered by any consequences thereof). Well, it would be safe for him to look up – her attention was surely distracted now by the task of balancing.

Two seconds.

His eyes rose to her middle as her middle slid to his left. He stared into her clothing, but did not see it. He took a breath. Time slowed. Why did time slow? he thought, clearly and calmly, musing as if his mind were an island, floating somewhere away from everything – which it was, suddenly, as his senses had become saturated, had filled up and fallen away from his conscious. He could feel the cool misty haze brushing against his skin, the hair on his head twitching as particles of the dead-still morning air flowed softly through it. The air slid through his parted lips and against the underside of his tongue, which was lightly pressed against the back of his front teeth. He could feel the groove between them, could taste the single grain of sugar stuck there by the pastry he had just finished. Everything was distinct, every sensation was perfectly packaged in the body; distilled and perceived from afar by the mind. A thunderous cloud of sound and smell invaded his nostrils and ears. It was rich and powerful, like mighty rushing waters, engine oil, asphalt, the roar of the speedway, the odor of the city, hints of smoke, burning…and into the thick brew a faraway siren cut sharply.

One and three-fourths seconds.

How strange, he thought. What could possibly be happening? he thought, with detached curiosity. His mind was quiet, empty, clear and silent, almost ringing.

His eyes had become fixed on her hands, hands that swung wildly around as she flailed to maintain balance. Suddenly they became clear. He could see the soft outline of veins on the back of her right hand, the hard outline of tensed tendons. Her fingers were frozen, extended. He saw them vividly and distinctly, as though she stood five feet away, offering her hand in greeting.

One and one-half seconds.

His eyes rose to her neck, which was lined with delicate sinew as she pulled her jaw tight. Sparkles of sweat or dew shone at the edges of her neck as beams of sunlight reflected around its profile. She was so close. His mind was so clear, so apart. Her neck was like a picture, which he could gaze upon for hours. He felt his eyes as they moved in their sockets. How strange, he thought, again, for the there was so much time to think. He listened hard to the silence, the hollow ringing. It was immensely quiet. His sight was not affected by depth – everything was in focus. He watched as the sharp outline of a streetlight post slid across his field of vision, disappearing behind her neck and reappearing on the other side.

She was still stumbling, still trying to regain balance. Stop trying, he thought, allowing concern into his mind for the first time. Take the fall. You don't want to fall out in the dirty street; I can help if you get a little banged up (he had taken a first-aid class once); who are you? He formed the words completely, deliberately. His mind was so clear.

One second.

His eyes met her face. He perused it, explored it. Twenty-three? Twenty-four? She had those small lines of concern, of worldly experience. She surely must have been a bit younger than him!...but she looked tired, worn-out. Is this the same girl who was just doing the dance? he thought. How strange, how...

But suddenly he could think no more. The ringing in his mind grew fiercely loud and the barriers between the mind and senses crumbled, flooding his whole being with feeling. His skin burned, his tongue was dry, a storm exploded in his head. He could not think. A thunderous grayness enveloped his mind. The words which had flowed so airily through it were buried in the flood. He could not hear, he could not feel, he could not smell.

He could still see. He could do nothing but see,

and watch; his whole being numbed with a buzzing paralysis. Everything now unfolded like a movie. His vision narrowed, flattened, focused only on her face, her face which seemed inches from his now, turned so that he could see both eyes.

One-half second.

Her eyes filled his vision. Her eyes did not meet his. He watched as they widened, staring at something far beyond him. The pupils dilated into large, black holes. He could see the blood vessels around them, shooting out into the whites, pulsating. He could do nothing but watch.

One-quarter second.

Her eyes grew dull, the lids relaxing together in surrender. Rolling lazily to the side, they met his. And stopped. He was awash in sensation. This was it. Everything froze. They held the stare.

Zero seconds.

The square-paneled mirror cut into his field of vision from the left, gradually blocking her face from view. One eye. No eyes. The stare interrupted, his focus released. He now saw everything. A body. A mirror where a head should be. A truck attached to the mirror. Sirens. The buzz was unbearable.

Pop.

It was one noise, a single moment of contact. No complexity. Shattered bone, smashed tissue, horrifying, gruesome, tragic – everything left to imagination. Just a simple pop. A faint pink puff appeared to the right side of the mirror. Her hands jerked. Her feet lifted from the ground. She flipped like a tossed doll, arms flung over-head. The truck had passed. As she spun, he caught a glimpse of what had been her face. There was no more face. The nose was gone, eyes were buried behind flaps of raw red-and-white tissue. One more flip. This time her extended arms brushed the pavement and the continued rotation of her strung-out body brought her legs smash-ing to the ground. She crumpled, falling forward onto her knees, chest, and finally her face. What had been a face. The hands hit the ground last. The fingers on the right one twitched.

The roar in his head subsided, his mind was released and his senses returned to something near normal. The stale air in his lungs tumbled out and he began to breathe again. He could think again. I feel nothing, he thought, testing his emotions. Something was bound to grab him. He wept openly at funerals, he liked to feel as though he had a soft spot for tragedy. But there was nothing. He should have been horrified, but there was no horror. Only numbness.

That was the worst thing I've ever seen, he thought. That was so incredibly sad, he thought. He formed the words. He passed them one by one through his mind. He was not sad. He was numb. That was hilarious, he thought. She…she deserved it! he though. No effect. Numb.

The siren stopped. Everything was silent. He looked around, at the sky, at the street, at the body, at the policeman, at the bright blood droplets scattered on the sidewalk in front of him. Then the silence broke, as people appeared from doorways and cars. They'll ask me about it, he thought. I ought to give an account, he thought. Is it illegal for a witness to leave the scene? he thought.

There was no emotion. He did not care. He was numb. He turned around and began walking. Took the first alley to his left, walked for two blocks, turned left again, bypassed the accident scene, returned to Broad Street, and continued on toward his destination. Nobody stopped him. He reached the hospital and entered, finding himself at length in the right ward on the right floor at the right nurses' station. No one was there. A growing feeling of discomfort began to worm into his stomach, pressing up against his chest, as the sourness of what lay ahead mingled with the unpleasantness of the young day's events.

May I help you, a bustling nurse offered, striding from the corridor on the right. Yes, he told her, she could help. He was here for the baby.

The baby? She eyed him curiously.

Yes, the baby, he thought. Do I really have to call it MY child, my precious child, darling boy or something like that? My child...MY child...his chest tightened.

Your name? she was saying, eyes glued to a clip-board-bound form which he had rather illegibly filled out over a week ago.

Adam Smith, he told her. Yeah, I know, like the economist. The nurse scribbled something down, dropped the clipboard on the desk. Right down there, she point-ed, right-hand corridor, last room on the left, door closed, lights off. That's where he would find the baby, sleeping in his crib, the IV taken out...now if he would excuse her she was done with her shift and simply couldn't stand the habitual tardiness of her replacement and I know it's not the rules but I gotta at least step outside...

She pulled a cigarette pack from a pocket and turned toward the elevators.

He mumbled something and walked down the cor-ridor. The last door on the left was open, and the light was on. But hadn't she said—? Glancing through some pa-perwork in a wall-mounted document holder by the door, the situation became clear – wrong baby! She had been in quite a hurry...he checked the paperwork across the hall.

Right baby. Ah.

This door was closed, shade down, light off. He reached for the handle, his heartbeat quickening. This was the moment, he thought. The first moment of the rest of...

No, no, not yet…wait for the nurse…let me just sit down! He stepped back, turned around. There was a chair in the wrong baby room. The light was on. The window shade was raised. His heart eased its pace. He walked in and stood still. Tried to think. Couldn't think. Feeling weakly mischievous he quietly closed the door, lowered its shade, flicked the light off, and sat down. There was a clock on the wall – the time was 7:32. He closed his eyes, drew in a deep, tired sigh of relief and let it slide slowly out through his teeth.

The truck didn't even stop! he recalled suddenly, with a – but there was no anger. There was no feeling. There was nothing. How could there be nothing?

The boy awoke with a start, reaching hastily for the backpack beside him. Opening it, he felt inside. Good. It was still there. The boy stood, stretching, exhaustion flooding his head. He collapsed back into the seat.

What a night it had been! I've got to do this again sometime…the thought trailed off. The boy leaned toward the aisle, looked ahead to the front section of the bus. Feet, people, lots of people. They were shuffling, murmuring.

Occasional bursts of laughter shot out over the hum, painfully out of step with the subdued energy of the early morning commute. He closed his eyes. It had been so quiet at night, so – so serene, that was the word! Serene and also surreal, maybe…right? Something like that.

The whole thing had started yesterday after school. Mother had come down in the car to pick him up from the bus stop…Mother, always being so nice, but so dumb. She thought if she did stuff, if she just did things for him it would be ok. Oh, she wanted him to be happy. She would love to make him *happy*. She wouldn't try to understand, though, he had thought, as he watched her blank smile through the windshield. It just wasn't going to happen, probably not even after tomorrow. She didn't want to understand, she didn't want to get it; she just wanted him to be happy. So stupid!

He had stood in the hot sun, feeling the heat welling up under his black shirt and navy jeans. He was not uncomfortable. Well, maybe a little, but it didn't bother him. It's like a symbol, he thought, of how things are. Burning up inside…ha. Dumb. But true, kind of…

It was Thursday afternoon. He was scheduled to stay at a Jimmy's house. A barely approved friend, but practically an angel next to the unapproved friends… besides, as parental reasoning went, this one lived in an apartment just a mile from school so there would be no Oops, I missed the school bus.

That's how he had reasoned, asking for their approval. His mother was soft, and of course she had agreed to the sleepover straight away (oh, maybe he would just be *happy* if she let him do what he asked). Father made a show, gave a stern eye, then a wary eye, then an almost-sad eye, but had finally given in. He was going to give in all along, the boy knew, for he just wanted Mother – he just wanted everyone to be *happy*. Real stuff didn't matter. What happened and what went on and how things were didn't matter. It only mattered that they could all be *happy*.

Well, he wasn't. How could you be happy when things were so bad, he wondered, brooding silently as she drove him into town later that afternoon. He was in sixth grade now, one of the youngest in his class at barely eleven. He was picked on, sure, but that wasn't the worst thing. Yeah, it hurt. Yeah, he may have cried a little the first week. But that wasn't it. He could have handled *that*. The other kids were just foolish. Dumb and jealous. He was the smart one in his class, after all, always had been, and the other kids knew it (somehow – it's not like he showed off, especially in class).

But that wasn't the real problem. See, it was more like – well, there was that eighth grade girl, Katie Jones, basically the star of the middle school. He passed her in the hallway once a day. She always wore a collared shirt and those preppy khaki pants, always was surrounded by a giggling clump of girlfriends. She had never missed an A, was the student council president, captain of the Academic Quiz Team, had won some essay contests, had probably won a bunch of other contests…whatever. He didn't care. But it was like she had the whole world at her fingertips. All the regular kids liked her. The teachers in the hall looked at her so approvingly. Katie Jones could do no wrong. But even so, it hadn't really bothered him at all until last week. Until last week he had just assumed she was smart like him. Smart and motivated and eager to conform to everything she was supposed to be. He could be that way too, if he wanted, which he didn't.

But all that wasn't really it, either. The real problem was that he was himself, and he was rejected. Completely misunderstood. By everyone. Parents, teachers, the other kids, even his so-called friends – no one understood him at all, or even cared to try. His friends, the ones that called themselves his friends…he couldn't stand them. They were the losers, the kids who would slide through school wearing black, leaving their hair long, moping and pretending to think deep thoughts, pretending they were really smart and serious…they were useless. But they were all he had on his side (especially since he now got treated by everyone else like he was one of them). Just by being himself he had become their hero. Why? What did he do wrong? He didn't act like the rest of them, did he? He didn't wear the same clothes, didn't talk about the same depressing stuff...well, maybe some, but that's not ALL he talked about, right?

Ok, so he was different. He was the smartest, the most intelligent kid in sixth grade and all the losers knew it it. The teachers knew it. All the other kids knew it. But it didn't matter. He just didn't fit. Being smart was a curse. He could never act like Katie Jones. He hated school, he hated classes; there was just nothing for him there. There was nothing for him anywhere. He had felt it all along. And then last week...

But that had to wait. He could think about it later, when there was time. There would be a lot of time. Now, he needed to focus on the plan.

Reflections of the afternoon sun glinted off the windows of oncoming traffic as his mother silently drove into the city. He slipped his earphones in and turned on his CD player. He would get a new digital music player for Christmas, he knew, because he had mentioned it once. Mother would give him what he wanted, just like she had given him the CD he now listened to. It was his new favorite: the band played metal, harder than anything the other kids listened to, and the lyrics were awesome! Still, he had felt embarrassed as his mother had handed it to him, conspicuous "Parental Advisory" sticker and all. She would do anything.

The first song crashed in with grinding guitar chords over a heavy, thumping rhythm.

You coward dogs, you crooked thieves
You lunatics are all to blame
You push me hard I'll pull a gun
Pull a trigger, make a name

The song was so intense, so raw. He felt a surge of delicious anger every time he listened, growing hotter as the singer's growls rose into a frantic scream for the final chorus…and there sat Mother, so unaware. He couldn't stand it. He looked at her passive face, studying the traffic, so completely unaware, so – so stupid!

Ah, but that would be to his advantage today…

The thought did not help. It was not comforting. He looked out the window, staring at the drivers of the cars they passed. A businessman in a luxury sedan, a farmer and wife in a truck, a mother with a car-seated baby in a minivan, a college girl with dopey sunglasses in a Beetle…

You'll remember to call, his mother was saying. Yes, yes, he would remember. Good, and she gave him that stupid, annoying, hopeful gaze.

She dropped him off at the curb, handed him his backpack, drove away slowly until Jimmy opened the apartment door. She waved, probably. He didn't look.

The boy knew what to expect: Jimmy was good for one thing – video games. The apartment was stocked with all the systems and the two of them got to play all the new releases, because Jimmy's mom was single and busy and Jimmy was an only child.

At school, he talked to Jimmy often enough, at least once a day, but only about video games. That was all there really seemed to be. Jimmy was good for one thing. They probably wouldn't have anything in common otherwise. Oh well. Today he would have to be good for something else. There were no new videogames at the apartment this week, so Jimmy pulled out a classic, one of the original 3D shooters. They played for a couple hours, taking turns and trying to unlock all the cheats. It was fun. The boy enjoyed it. The blocky 3D models, the exploitable glitches, the old-school bright red crosshair. It was entertaining, a change of pace. But his mind inevitably wandered to the task ahead.

Jimmy went to the bathroom. The boy looked at his watch. Seven o'clock. It was time. The boy stood, grabbed his backpack, and tiptoed passed the kitchen to the living room, where a large dresser stood. There was no sign of Jimmy's mom. She hadn't been around all afternoon, in fact. He reached up to the top drawer and slid it open. He froze as it squeaked loudly. Waited…nothing. Barely breathing, he felt inside. The cloth-wrapped bundle was there. He grabbed it, put it in his backpack, closed the drawer (squeak), and rushed back into the game room. The toilet flushed. He pulled his cell phone out of his pocket and held it to his ear. Watching from the corner of his eye as Jimmy reentered the room, he theatrically stomped his foot, grimaced and shoved the phone back into his pocket.

It worked. He explained that something had been found out and so he was now in minor trouble (there was no need for specifics, as it was expected among his so-called friends that they would often be at odds with parents), and that his mother was storming over to pick him up at 7:30; Jimmy believed it, of course. Jimmy even mentioned that his mom would not be home from her dinner meeting until 8, so – ha ha – she would never have any idea that a friend had been over at all.

So Jimmy was good for something, thought the boy. He himself had never invited a friend over without telling his mother. Not that he really ever had anyone over. Losers…

At 7:30 the boy pretended to receive another call. That was Mother. See ya. He shut the door in Jimmy's face. Jimmy would probably be looking out the window, so he pulled out his phone yet again and craned his neck, as if looking down the road. Remembering Mother's earlier request, he pressed the call button.

Yes, he told her, they were having a good time. No, no problems. School in the morning, yes, I know. Ok, bye. He turned the phone off but kept it to his ear, ducking and sidestepping as if trying to see through traffic. After a while he glanced at the apartment windows behind him. Jimmy was not in sight. He felt a little silly. Well thanks anyway, he thought. Hopefully I won't need you again.

The boy turned toward the nearest bus stop, checking his pockets for correct change. He needed to be smooth, mature. The sun was now low behind, casting a long shadow before him. He breathed deeply, noticing the pungent, exciting smell of the city like he never had before. Standing up straight, feeling tall, he raised his gaze to the darkening blue sky ahead.

Soon he reached the bus stop. At 7:45, bus number 12, one of those two-segment buses, pulled up (artic… articulated? Yeah, that was it). He got on in the front, walked quickly down the aisle, almost to the second segment, and sat down in the only empty row. Yes, this was the right one. Bus number 12. Good.

He put the backpack under his seat, put his earphones in and sighed: smooth sailing so far.

He wished he had thought to bring more than just one CD. Oh well.

Let 'em know they're all to blame
Don't you know you're all to blame

It is time to think. I am going to think. Adam closed his eyes, quieting his mind.

He opened them again. Indirect morning light from the window cast a soft glow into the otherwise darkened room. It was a white, clinical room, distinguishable as a children's setting only by a wallpaper band of purple elephants running around up by the ceiling. Besides the baby crib, furnishings included the chair he sat on, a clock, a wheeled metal cart in the corner with nothing on it, a slowly spinning ceiling fan, and the closed folding doors of a closet opposite the window. It seemed quite bare for a hospital room (overflow?). The baby slept quietly on a medical crib near the window, covered, except for its head, by a thick gray blanket. The blue beanie-capped head (cute, he supposed) rested gently on a folded square of bright white cloth.

A soft, familiar hum from above slowly filled his ears; he allowed his eyes to drift upward to the lazily spinning fan and was seized by a powerful nostalgia: quiet afternoon naps of boyhood; floating without a care on the border of dreams; lying comfortably in the half-light which diffused through soft brown curtains, filtered from the eternal sun, the bright and endless sun! He had but to rise from the bed and run, to bound out into the hot blue day and seize all the joy of young life: looking back with pleasure, looking forward with excitement, all the while drinking in the thrill and release of now – oh, to be there again, to love the NOW, to lie in bed with the smell of Mother cooking in the kitchen, the quiet rustle of the fan; so secure in the filtered glow of the dazzling world outside, the world at his fingertips, the world which now—

He shook his head. There was no use. Sometimes the thoughts would wind themselves up and he would get lost, lost for hours, drifting from one image to the next, for better or worse. Worse, usually. Always, according to *her*…

Of course, today was different. Had he not just witnessed the most dramatic, the most powerful moment of his twenty-five years? He searched his emotions, finding still the numbness. He concentrated on it, stared at the wall. Numbness. Give me something, he thought. Something appropriate, something sharp and penetrating – disgust, horror, sadness, whatever. I don't care. Give me something!

A minute went by. Nothing. This would not do.

He needed a reaction, a gut impulse to go along with that mangled face, just to put his mind right – *just ta feel satisfied*...Bob Dylan? Maybe? You know, he thought, in context a well-written song lyric can express such clarity, can cut deeper than a whole paragraph of precisely placed words...

Ah! Stop it! He shook his head again. Death. Death, he repeated. I have seen death, violent and sudden. Death as plainly as it comes. I have seen a girl removed from this life, removed from parents, sisters, friends – he looked at the baby – children...face smashed, blood spattered all over the street. At my feet, all over the sidewalk! Drunk and happy, maybe. Maybe just happy. Maybe the happiest moment of her life, then a stumble, a second of shock, and that's it. Carried off to...

Huh. Carried off. Why did he think that? Why did he say that? It irked him – borrowing a phrase from religion, from the tired, foolish religion of his family. He knew right where it came from, too. Grandmother's funeral, his first, ten years ago; that eloquent minister, conjuring the perfect emotions from his audience: Though we mourn, today she has been carried off to a sweet, sweet paradise where sorrow has no purchase!

Yes, carried off. He had been all in line with it then. Silent tears rolling over a bittersweet smile, grief tempered beautifully by assurances of the heaven-bound.

Yeah, yeah, yeah. That was back in the early, impression-able days – they had been so easy! Ah, but it was all a lie, all a scam. He had learned better since then, had learned the truth – well, maybe not the truth, no, that was a fool-ish thing to claim – but he had certainly learned the lie. Religion – all of it – was of no use to the thinking man, to anyone, especially here and now in this postmodern world without barriers or hard rules or limits. Why did so many otherwise reasonable people hang on so desperately?

Aw, come on. The mind was rambling again. Quit running in these circles! he chided. He looked at the clock. 7:45 – well, he wouldn't be missed until at least 11…no, time was no matter. It was the manner of the question he had proposed – he hated those patronizing rhetorical ques-tions: oh, how is it that the fools are so foolish? And re-ally, the underlying annoyance was that he had slipped into language that was not his own, had allowed the words of some self-righteous moral-high-ground-claiming pseudo-philosophical muser to pass through his lips.

Ha, he sniffed, almost snickered aloud. It's fun-ny how things always come together. But of course, this was the whole point, the very answer to the question with which he had so offended his sensibility: using the words of another, the thoughts and ideas of another to cover gaps in one's own thinking. That, of course, was the essence of religion.

Yes, it was so very clear (and he had thought through all this before, making the offending question all the more useless). Religion was the great stopgap, the (no, no, not opiate not crutch, find something of your own!) – the great veil that covered all holes in the mind and spirit. Religion was a whole system of the thoughts and ideas of others, convenient and battle-tested (he smirked at the cliché's connotative depth). Don't know something? Get thee some religion! Don't feel good? Ditto. At least, that's how it worked in this country. Religion for the masses was self-help and backless inspiration. Nothing more. He'd watched the preachers on television; on trips home from college he'd even begun really listening to the Methodist minister at his parents' five-thousand member church. And here was the simple, shallow recipe: take a few inspiring phrases and add the right keywords – GOD wants you to be successful, JESUS showed you how to feel better about yourself, use the BIBLE for your daily encouragement! Fa la la la la and all that. Joy and peace and happiness, for those without the tools to build such things for themselves, to find harmony by the power of their own intellects.

Of course, it must be admitted, religion worked differently elsewhere in the world. There seemed to be a correlation between the sum of oppression, ignorance, and misery with the dominance of religion (maybe there was some kind of index he could create? – this was beginning to get entertaining). The bigger the gaps in the mind, the more trampled-down the spirit (semantics – the spirit was of course just a facet of the mind), the more religion asked and the more it promised. The drug became stronger, more addictive, more sinister as earthly circumstance became direr. Give us your money, and things will be better for you in this life! No hope for this life? Sacrifice it for God and things will be better after you die!

No, religion was simply not something he needed, not something anyone needed. Why draw your mental sustenance from historical obscurity and archaic rules when you can THINK! – when you can reason, when you can argue, when you can study things for what they are and not worry about some fabricated concept of Jesus or Allah or whatever peering over your shoulder.

But perhaps he was being a little cruel. He had been fortunate; this whole country was fortunate. Elsewhere in the world there was little true relief from the infliction of modern life, from the plague of ignorance and dullness and uselessness. Who was he to sneer at those who not only had nothing beside religion but COULD have nothing beside religion to get them through the days, the weeks, the years? No, it was not fair to expect otherwise. It was just a sad reality (sad, he thought without feeling).

But all these people over here, in this land of opportunity, all these decently educated people!…if they could only see clearly what they REALLY were getting out of their religious experience. If they just thought about the reality of what they truly asked and wanted from it all…!

Adam sat back, sighed deeply. That was enough. He'd been through this before, come to the same conclusion. I need to save it for a real argument, with someone other than myself, he thought. Need to stop turning it over and over, like – like basting my brain with the same stuff that self-righteous moral-something pseudo-philosophical…muser, did I call him? Yeah – the same stuff that guy was on. Ha…okay, done.

He forced his eyes to wander, to find something new, and they quickly settled on the baby. Here he had been chattering about in his mind for…all right, not that long, but still. There was real life, sleeping right there in front of him, and here he had been, in another world…

The baby. What about the baby? He was sitting in a room with a sleeping baby. It wasn't his baby. It wasn't *her* baby. *She* was at home, waiting for Adam and that child across the hall. But that was not now. Now, there was just this baby. It looked a lot like his baby: a few months old, similar size, similar shape, maybe a little lighter-skinned. Maybe a little easier on medical bills. Babies. They were really all the same, these babies. No experience, no memory, pretty much inert. *Baby, baby, baby…*

Just a man and a baby in a room together, silent.

So. Whose baby? Would someone soon be barging in to claim it?

A thought: what if...? What if, thought Adam, what if there was no one? What if that girl in the street was the mother of this baby, and she was dead? And the father, naturally, had never been there? The baby was alone. He spun the image, pretended, imagined, shut his eyes.

Nothing. Numb. He imagined his death, *her* death, the baby across the hall. Nothing. That baby would grow, would never know, would miss nothing...numb.

Numb, numb, numb! He pressed the back of his head against the wall, grasping frantically for a feeling: he pictured Broad Street, he saw the face, the smashed-up, shattered face of the dead woman, as her body lay mangled and her blood seeped lifelessly out into the street; now she was in a coffin, reconstructed waxy plaster face shining luridly through the makeup, and here was her mother – his mother, his father, his grandmother – staring and staring and seeing not even the face of the dead but only the cold hands of the dead folded over the hollow chest of the dead below this horrid mask of the never-living, and feeling down to their bones the overwhelming emptiness of knowing that the face they cannot see before them is the face they will never, never see again!

A twinge. He felt a twinge, a catch in his breathing.

The image, just the last one, stung, it hurt. Strange relief swept over him, a half-smile appeared on his face. Yes, it was real now. He had seen death. He had really seen death. Real, raw, deep, permanent.

It was odd, this death. Really brought one face-to-face with reality, with what it all means, where it all leads. None of those angel choruses and heavenly bands...

He had gone to college a Methodist. First year, in philosophy class, the professor had asked: What religion do you identify with (and if you don't want to tell, that's ok)? But the girl to his left had smiled and said Christian and so he said Methodist.

And after that he began to read. And think. And the I Am a Methodist fell somewhere back into the deep recesses of the I Am Adam Smith and soon was completely disconnected from the I Am Adam Smith, which grew marvelously in its newfound independence. The holes in the mind were filling, the spirit was in tune. Conversations with professors, conversations with students, conversations with himself: all religions met and overlapped in the same places, all filled the same gaps. All claimed something, none could be sifted out. That's not true, said one of his religious friends. But what would you expect a self-identifying Christian to say, smiled the professors of religion. And he had taken it all under advisement. But one night he sat up, thinking. Using his own words. What does religion give? What does religion promise? What do I need from religion?

And that last question had been enough. He needed…nothing. He needed nothing from it. What I need, he had thought, is to think the right way about things, to see things for what they are, to remove the distracting sentiments, to find out the truth and not concern myself with that which cannot be ascertained, that which can only be chased blindly after.

To think the right way. Yes, he now thought the *right way*. He had perhaps taken wrong turns, made errors, but it could all be reversed, all was possible. His thought was liquid; he could pour it over anything, any problem, and it would feel the contours and slip into all the cracks. The world needed true thinkers; he had only to stand up.

He stood up. The sun streamed in for the first time, casting two golden panels on the white wall to his left. This was life. Life was outside, life was now, life was thought, and his thought was good! He pushed away the baby, he pushed away the death. Those were the bookends. And I am not there! he thought. I am alive, I think, I can do, it is time! It's time to unleash the mind, to capture all that can be captured, to inherit the pure satisfaction of being.

Yes, he would turn, walk over there, get that baby – his baby, go home to *her*, and she would not be able to drag him down! He would leave them at home and walk out into the sun, under the bright blue sky, feeling the pleasure of yesterday and the promise of tomorrow and knowing that he had found the key, that he could THINK.

In two great steps he was at the door handle. He grabbed it. Yes, he would march right down to the depot and tell them he was…well, no, he couldn't quite do that, not with the baby, the medical bills. But after he started writing, or maybe after he found a better job…

He stared at his hand on the door handle. He could hear the whispering of the fan behind him and a distant honking outside and he felt his energy draining, seeping out of his face, out of his heart, right into the floor. Into his head swam images of the depot, of the mind-numbing work, of the large, identical boxes; shipments of clothes, of food, of books – oh, the massive shipments of popular books! They would go to the bookstores, shelved like fool's gold alongside the full breadth of authorship, the millions of pages, the words of others that went forever unread; words born of visions small and great, shallow and deep, plain and fantastic – and all so vastly unimportant, unseen. Into his head marched the endless times he had picked up a pen, the endless times he had had something to say. One line, two lines…and then the words were gone, the power was gone, the heat was gone.

And now this moment had soaked away into reality. Reality: he would get his baby, put it in the stroller *she* had left here overnight. He would walk to the apartment and *she* would be there, asking about the morning and about the weather and he would look into her eyes and see that they could never really meet his own and he would collapse on the sofa and watch television, which he hated. And he would go back to his work at the depot, where they paid him too well to walk away, where he would stumble through each day, dreaming and wishing, knowing that his thought and his words were his own, knowing that they would never be heard.

Adam stepped backwards. He made a quarter-turn left and shuffled sideways, back to the chair. He sat down softly and clasped his hands together, staring at the wall. It was 8:07.

The sun was almost down. Soft shadows, framed by the dull red haze of the setting sun, flowed hypnotically through the interior of the bus as it turned, right, right, left, right…

The boy stared into the shadows. It had all come together last week. Before that…well, the kids were stupid, he was totally different from everyone, and nobody liked him but the losers – but maybe things would get better. His mother told him that, at least. Whatever good that was. He hated when she picked up on his bad moods. She never picked up on anything useful. Couldn't she see that he didn't want to be bothered? That bothering him and trying to help him when he didn't want it was worse than nothing at all? No, she couldn't. But she had said that the older you get the more respect you get for being smart and unique. Unique. Sure, whatever. That's what all parents probably told their kids. Still, he had grudgingly allowed the notion of future respect to lift his spirits. Just enough to hold out some kind of hope.

But last week. Last week, Wednesday, after school…well, the whole day had been terrible, really, from the third step off the bus in the morning, when he had accidentally run into an older kid, an eighth-grader they called Millsy. Danny Mills or something. Millsy played football, and you didn't mess with him. It hadn't been the boy's fault at all, because he had been walking straight ahead and Millsy had sort of backed up in his path. But of course he had been knocked aside, almost falling down, stumbling awkwardly to retain balance, and Millsy had called out Whoa, look out there little man! in his general direction, loud enough for the whole schoolyard to hear. And things like that happened every day…

Every day the boy tried to make it through his first

class without speaking, without getting called on, trying to be as invisible as he could. You ought to speak up more, the teacher would tell him. But what did he care? It was a stupid class. Advanced History or something. A showcase for kids that could somehow care about useless things, about whatever they were told to care about. Supposedly it was part of the gifted curriculum, but he couldn't see how the class itself had anything to do with being smart; maybe you couldn't be stupid, but you definitely didn't need to be smart. The tests were easy. Straight from the book. The quizzes were easy. The knowledge was useless. There was nothing here for him, nothing at all.

The teacher, a younger woman, was always mothering the class, delighting in right answers, putting on a disappointed-puppy-dog face when the answers were wrong. She was very nice. She cared. He couldn't stand her.

What factors do you think might have brought about the decline and fall of the empire? she asked today, as the end of the period neared.

This again…a perfect example of what was wrong with school, with classes, with all this so-called learning.

The teacher would ask these What-Do-You-Think questions about things that the kids knew nothing about, apart from what they might have read in the textbook. And then when they answered (and if you read ahead in the book you could always find the correct answers) she would act as though they had just thought of something significant, as if they really KNEW something, as if they somehow understood what they were talking about!

The boy had in fact read a book about today's subject last summer, a dusty volume he had found on a shelf in a corner of the attic. Actually, the book had described a single battle on a single day that had been very important in the eventual decline of the empire. The story was complicated, a little hard to follow; there were all these interactions between the different armies and different generals and different political groups...the boy had come to realize just how little of the subject he knew, even after reading the book cover to cover. How little you could really learn about something from one book, how much less you could learn from one class period...

Maybe other countries became more advanced? That was Robert in the back row, always trying to go first, to get the simple answer before it was taken by someone else.

Yeah, and the empire's own army didn't keep up with the times! John S. acting so confident, only speaking up when the answers were obvious. Loser.

Very good! the teacher gushed. You're right, both of you! And what else?

Maybe...uh, I don't know if this is right, but didn't

communication between provinces break down because the empire got too big to govern? That was front-row Suzy, always reading ahead, always correct, always acting sickeningly unsure of herself.

Excellent! the teacher cried. Suzy, you ought to be more confident...

What a joke. The boy turned away, stared out the window, sank into his own daydream...oh, to BE there, to know what it was really like, standing under a bright blue sky on the packed dirt path between two green fields, an ancient village built of gray stone in the distance, no sound but the waving of the grass in the breeze, no smell but fear as the barbarian horde sweeps silently down from the north...thinking about life and death, the great distance between today and tomorrow, one year and the next, how you could never explain, how so much changes...

The bell rang. Whatever.

It was such a waste: forty-five minutes of kids being lectured and then asked to add to what they'd just heard, as if they would have anything useful to say; as if it were possible that a bunch of idiot kids chattering about stuff they didn't understand would magically cause new knowledge to appear. And the teacher praised them for their nonsense, so they could feel accomplished, feel like they were smart. Everyone could be smart: memorize certain parts of the textbook and we'll pretend you understand the subject. Learning. It wasn't about the truth or understanding or who was smarter or more thoughtful. Suzy read ahead, Suzy got to be the smart one. What was the point? Suzy hadn't learned anything other than how to please the teacher, to play a simple game well without even realizing it. He imagined Suzy as an adult: Do you know? she asked her husband (ha, and who would THAT be?), as they strolled down the sidewalk, do you know why the empire fell...

What was he doing here? Was school supposed to interest him? He had tried to say something to his parents about it, tried to let on, just a little bit, as they sat around the dinner table, but...Why don't you skip a grade? Mother had suggested. Yes, said Father. Maybe that would make you happier, put you in a better place...

And that had been that. No. No way.

The music stopped suddenly, startling the boy, as he had grown practically unaware of it. He held up his CD player in the dimming light (it was quickly darkening outside) – out of battery. No problem. He had another pair in his backpack somewhere...but it was probably time to make his next move, anyway. He scanned the aisle, up and down. There were still a lot of people in the front section of the bus. Not as many in the back. He looked at his cell phone. 8:25. A pinching nervousness began to grip his stomach. He had never been on a bus at night. He had never been alone at night. He had never even taken a dare...

But this was the moment – this had to be it. The bus had come to a stop, and at least half of the passengers stood. He glanced toward the back section. Lots of movement there, too. The boy reached under his seat, grabbed the backpack, and stood. In the confusion he slipped quickly to the back section and ducked into the first seat on his left – the right side of the bus. The perfect hiding spot. He had made the discovery several months ago, on a day trip with his parents to the museum. You sit in this seat, on this bus, right behind the unusual metal panel stretching from floor to ceiling; slide all the way to the right, and there's no way for the driver to see you. You scrunch down a little, and the passengers behind you can't see you, either. Hopefully. He flicked his eyes nervously up and down the aisle. Yet, he now noted, even when you slid all the way to the window there were a few seats, in the front section and across the aisle, that were still in plain view, including – what the…?!

There was Nick, that idiot Nick and couple of his friends, sitting right where he had been before. They must have just gotten on. The pinching in his stomach returned, as he hoped desperately that they wouldn't turn and see him. He flipped the hood of his sweater over his head and turned toward the window.

Of all the classes, Nick just had to be in P.E. with him. P.E. was his second class on Wednesday. He hated it, naturally. You had to change into gym clothes, and he always felt so out of place, so…so undressed, standing there in the locker room with his pale skinny legs sticking awkwardly out of those little shorts. It seemed like all the other kids in class were athletic, were tan – oh, maybe not, but at least they were having fun. He could imagine having fun, too, if he were better at sports, more popular, bigger, stronger. But he wasn't. At least showers weren't required…

But that stupid Nick – Nick was like a bully. It's not that he ever DID anything – stole money, beat people up – anything that really hurt other kids, but…well, he was just not nice. His friends, too. It was one of those little groups. They weren't the popular kids, but they weren't near the bottom of the ladder either. They did their own thing, had their own jokes. Nobody messed with them. And they just weren't nice.

And they all just had to be in P.E. with him. That day, last week, the boy had been minding his business, walking toward the locker room toilets. He saw the motion to his right but couldn't avoid it, didn't really get what was going on, until – flip, he felt a quick tug at the corner of his shorts and there they were, crumpled down around his ankles. Warm blood seeped up into his face as he jerked awkwardly to a standstill (stupid! he had thought, why can't you play it cool?) and grabbed wildly for his shorts. A few joyful shrieks and Nick's low-pitched laugh and at least one ohhhhhhhhhhhh! sounded out around him, and the boy knew he had to save face somehow and so he turned and tried to look Nick in the eye and, managing to fix an angry stare somewhere between Nick's shoulder and chin, blurted out in his child's voice Fuck you. And Nick, grinning and turning inward to his friends as if the boy had become invisible, continued chuckling. The boy walked on to the toilets as if nothing had happened, staring straight ahead, listening as Nick's gravelly voice sounded out beneath the general merriment now echoing behind him.

It wasn't that he was really embarrassed or needed to be. It had just been the shorts, not the boxers. Kids knew that Nick and his friends were idiots. But to be the target, to be the one that Nick went after, and to be able to stand there and tell Nick off, right to his face, and for it to mean nothing…His throat constricted and he blinked away tears. He was smart, he was smarter than them all, but somehow he was so helpless. Nick could prey on him every day if he wanted. If Nick did that to one of the other kids and the kid said Fuck you to Nick, there might be a fight, honor at stake, a reason to stand up for oneself. But the boy could say anything to Nick in his child's voice and it would just bounce away like crumpled paper. He had no weight. His friends, the ones he hated, couldn't help. They had no weight, either. But they were just losers. He wasn't a loser – no, he was smart, he was the smartest! Why was it so hard, then?

He had walked from class to class that day, becoming more and more miserable. At lunch he sat with Jimmy, next to a couple of loser friends of Jimmy's. They were wearing those stupid t-shirts from that one store all the losers shopped at because they somehow believed it made them different; one of them even had a wristband (probably from the same store) with shiny plastic studs. Ridiculous. And he had to talk with them, and he had to talk with Jimmy, and he had to be with them and be seen with them and be counted as one of them because there wasn't anything else to do, anywhere else to be.

And finally the school day ended and he was about to head for the buses when his first-period teacher caught him and reminded him of his expected attendance at the afterschool leadership mentoring workshop. And she was so nice and she always gave him that mothering look of half-hope, half-disappointment and so he had let her shepherd him in to the auditorium.

The students had all been divided into groups, with one eighth grader and a few sixth graders in each. They were given topics to discuss, and the eighth graders were supposed to talk about their experiences and give advice. Something stupid like that. The boy wasn't interested. He wanted out. He looked from the front-right corner of the stage, where his group had been stationed, to the nearest exit, imagining a quick escape. Hop off the stage, a couple steps to the aisle, and…

Then he noticed Katie Jones. She was sitting in a chair in the front row, already babbling away to a rapt audience of sixth graders clustered in a tight semi-circle on the floor. He stared as a mixture of disgust and envy and cold anger washed over him. She was so perfect, did everything everyone wanted. Cared in all the right ways, in all the right places. I would never want to be like her, he thought, he told himself, over and over. But the jealousy just increased.

His own mentor was having a lively conversation about something completely off-topic with the rest of his group. Whatever. He couldn't stop watching *her*. She was probably as smart as him. I would never want to be like her, he repeated. But he couldn't look away. He watched her face, her expressions, the movements of her hands. He listened to her words.

And all at once it dawned on him: I am smarter than her. The thought was uninvited, totally unexpected. But it rang true. And the more he watched, the clearer it became.

The classes in eighth grade really get HARD, Katie Jones was saying. Like, in Algebra I study all the TIME, and I have a big paper due next Monday for English and…

He looked into her eyes as she continued, searching for the truth.

In sixth grade I probably studied or did homework for like an hour a night, but now it's way more, she said. But don't worry, you'll get through it. Middle school's a lot of fun and…

He suddenly felt very cold. He was looking at the best student in the school, the superstar, loved by all, hated by none. She would win at least half of the year-end academic awards (he would win none, of course, but it's not like he tried). And here she was, saying she studied an hour a night in sixth grade. And it was the truth, her eyes said it was the truth. He didn't study, he never studied. There was no doubt that he could get As, too, if he just half-paid attention in class. It was really that easy. But her eyes said it wasn't. Not for her. Not for the superstar, the one everyone loved.

She wasn't anything special. She wasn't a genius. She just played the game well. She just cared about the game, cared about the things she was supposed to care about. That was all she had, all she really had. Was that all it took?

The boy was smarter than Katie Jones. Way smarter. How could that be? Yet it was so obvious…and it didn't matter. Nobody cared. Nothing mattered.

That had been the turning point. Last Wednesday,

after school. It was so small, he realized, such a silly thing. He could never explain it, never tell it to anyone. It would sound so insignificant coming from his lips. No one would take him seriously. No one would understand. How could they? Tell me what makes you angry, the counselor would say. Everything, he would say, and then he would try to explain. Mmm, the counselor would smile, I think I can help…

At home that night the boy had pulled a bottle of sleeping pills from Mother's medicine cabinet. And then put them away. The image of Mother crying at his hospital bedside was so pathetic it made him want to vomit.

Instead, he was now here, on a bus, at 9:00 PM the next Thursday. This time he was in charge of things.

The dim but cold greenish-white interior lighting of the bus had come on. He raised his eyes to the front section, surprised to see that Nick was still there, alone. His friends had apparently gotten off; now he was sitting still, leaning casually against the window.

Fuckin' loser, the boy whispered. Fuck you. Tingles shot down his spine as he pushed the hard F sound between his upper teeth and lower lip. The word made him feel older, more serious, more dangerous. It was like opening a window into the interactions of adulthood, like you see in movies (he got to watch what he wanted, of course). People knew you meant business when you said it…fffuck. I'm gonna fuckin' kill you!

The boy imagined the little red crosshair from the video game he had played earlier. It drifted over to Nick's head. Pop. Headshot with the magnum. He leaned just a little to the left, peering around the panel. Could he hit the driver? Pop – the bus hit a bump. Missed. Pop. Haha, there it was, 'nother headshot.

The boy leaned back, slumping against the side of the bus. 9:00. It was going to be a long night. He changed the CD player's batteries and flipped it on again.

Let 'em know they're all to blame
Pull a trigger, make a name
Don't you know they're all to blame
Pull a trigger, make a name

Adam touched his fingertips lightly to his left temple, sliding them weakly through his hair until his forehead lay in the palm of his hand.

It had never been this bad. He had never felt this spent, this aimless, even after crashing out of that foolish euphoria he always allowed himself to build. He brought his other hand to his face, brought them both together around his nose and mouth and blew a slow stream of air into his palms.

He had to get out of this. He had to get away from the baby, from the death. He had to give it a night, sleep it off, wake up in the morning. Something!

He gripped the armrests of the chair and stood up, slowly. The usual pains: a dull grinding sensation between two vertebrae in his lower back, a sharp sting in his right knee, and three or four clicks in his left shoulder socket as he used the arm for leverage. Tightness pulled through his calves, hamstrings, and lower back. He felt lightheaded, unsteady.

I'm so old, he thought idly. On the downslope. Every day a little weaker. Every day a little slower, a little stiffer. The hair thinner. A little more clouded in thought, more forgetful…He let his mind drift on. And why not? There was no danger of further depression. He was already at the bottom.

Yes, they never told you it worked like this. When you were young you pushed ahead, you were told that you wanted to grow up, you were told That's a no-no! and there would be this happy time of adulthood where you would be able to do as you pleased in the powerful, sophisticated body and mind of a grown-up. And you believed it, and you wanted it! If you were a reasonably observant child (as he supposed he had been), you saw the medication commercials and picked up on the notion that after a long and fruitful Prime of Life, at maybe around 40 or 45 you would begin descending into the slow and mysterious Aging Process.

Nah. Didn't work that way. One day he had woken up, looked in the mirror, and realized that from now on he would always be grasping to remember the face of – not NOW, not 23 or 22 or whenever it had been, but of sometime before…maybe eighteen. Always looking back. And staring into the face of 23 or 22 he had perceived for the first time the inevitable downslope. He had looked at his hair. Thinner, just that little bit thinner than eighteen. His lips, the corners of his mouth. His chin. His eyes. Drooping, creasing, deepening; everything had begun the slow march downward.

It was cruel, he mused now. Officially cruel. There was no plateau. You spend your youth, speed, strength, excitement aiming for the goal – to learn and grow and rise up and burst through those teenage years, thundering out onto the lofty plateau of adulthood. But of course there was no plateau, and so you kept moving forward until suddenly you realized that the very best years, the very best body and mind was right behind you, right out of reach, just last year, last month, yesterday.

Your vitality, he thought. *And sex and sex and sex and sex.*

The drive, the excitement…*Does it matter?*

The thrill! *Jaded, faded…*

He hated that now he could talk about sex plainly, that he could think about it and dwell on it and not feel that nervous tingle. He'd been a good kid; he had passed through those years as a Methodist, listening to the rules, never going beyond a safe, affectionate kiss. He was looking forward, waiting. And then in college, even after learning to think, he had continued, looking forward still in the promise of simple true love, of saving himself for *her*.

And then he had looked in the mirror and felt the downslope, and all the enchantment, all the purity of purpose melted away into irresolute weakness. He had gone to a fraternity party (so it must have been 22), Unchained Melody swimming in his head, and had somehow made his way to a couch with that girl who always flirted with him. They had left, returned to his apartment, and in the ecstasy of the night he discovered the foolishness of all the sentimental ideals he had harbored.

And then the next morning he discovered the foolishness of last night's decision. The weight. The irreversibility. But it was alright, because he was on the downslope – *look at me...I'm in tatters* – and now the songs in his head had changed for good. It was alright, it was all part of being on the downslope.

They never did it again. There was a falling out, a few words of reconciliation at some point, and then school was done and he had come to the city.

Almost half a year later, right after his first promotion at the depot, he had met *her*.

The flower, the muse, the angel – she had been perfection at the start. They met in the city's hot spot for music and youth and entertainment – the district. He had been sitting on a café patio on an especially pleasant early October evening – all right, October 9th. Saturday. And you better not forget. Anyway, his table was near the outdoor stage and when the band arrived she had asked him, in an impossibly charming manner, whether or not he had any extra room at his table. Without waiting for a reply, laughing, she grabbed a chair and brazenly slammed her guitar case down on the table, and of course from then on it had been pure enchantment. When not singing perfect harmonies and plucking out simple but soulful acoustic melodies, she melted his senses from the stage with intoxicating smiles and winks. He had been utterly lost in her energy, her boldness, her face, her voice. In her essence was the revelation of his incompleteness. She was that which he needed, that which he had always needed.

After the music was over they sat at the table and talked for four hours. Four hours, and his infatuation grew into absolute adoration. They seemed two spirits in parallel; they believed the same things, looked to the same ideals, liked…well, surprisingly similar music. And aside from the rest, by any standard her beauty was exquisite.

Adam gazed through the sunlit window, smiling at the bittersweet memory. That night had been a momentary restoration of the purity he had earlier renounced – a new chance at first love. At the end of their conversation he had walked her home, and not entered. Standing alone, he had been flooded with the regret of error, of his just-barely-premature choice six months before. He tried to rationalize. The downslope…but there was no such thing in *her* presence. She was all energy, all life. Could *she* be the answer? Could *she* give me back the youth, the hunger, the joy? he had wondered.

And for a time it had worked. But love is blindness, of course. No, Adam thought. Foolishness is blindness. I was just foolish, expected too much.

For she was his equal in style alone, not substance. After the initial wave of magic attraction, when things became more domestic and the bonds more intertwined but less electric, they had begun to know each other, to search each other's minds. They spoke frequently: politics, religion, music, ideas, ideas! And on so much they agreed, but one day, much later on, they had been talking about gender roles (and it was appropriate, with the baby on the way and all)...

And what's wrong with the woman working and the man raising the baby? she was saying.

But you'd want to raise—

Oh, yes, I want to raise MY baby, but I'm just talking about the principle of it. She assumed he would agree, as he had before. It was all in fun, he could tell, just a little back-and-forth that would allow them to feel just that little bit more connected, allow her to feel more confident as they approached together the great unknown of child-rearing. But he had thought deeply about it, had imagined the baby resting in his arms. And then in her arms. And it was not the same.

Well, he had offered, he'd thought about it and there is something to be said for the idea that just as it can be destructive when hard gender roles are enforced by a society, so too might it might be possible for us to go too far the other way. For example, could you really argue that a society where women raised all the children would not be better off than…

But you say women and men are equal, should have equal opportunity, right?

Yes, but if you go at it from a certain angle—

She smiled half-playfully. As long as that's not YOUR angle…

And he had looked deep into her eyes and she did not meet him. There was a barrier, and she would go no deeper. For he could THINK, he could take any notion and pierce it with his reasoning and tear it down and search among the rubble for truth – but for her there was the ideal and its justification, in that order. The words of previous conversations descended upon him, illuminated anew by this cold realization: their minds, superficially in parallel, were forged from entirely different stuff.

Now, it was hard to imagine that he had taken so long to figure it out. Things descended after that, became torturous and backward, as his lust for her intermingled with his despair at their inevitable, eternal disconnect. She was like encountering the perfect college student, over and over, ideas in line with all that is appropriate and built on a foundation of thought that extends to exactly the right depth – and no further, lest it be shaken by some deeper disturbance.

A month and half after their first encounter, she had

decided to move in. He had been promoted again, and could support them both with ease. They slept together then, for the first time, on a bed tainted by nothing but the faint image of that other girl flickering dimly in his mind. Now there was a baby, by all accounts finally in good health. It was success. It was the dream.

Was it him? Had he done wrong? If only he had seen her more clearly…No, this is my life, this is what I must do. If only he had known early on…But what would I really have done differently? If only he had the nerve to…No, no, no! I will not be the problem, I will not be the cancer…

Success success success
Does it matter?

The song was really in his head. Fine…guess there will always be a space for *her* in my—

Noises. A scratching from the hall.

As from a daze he started, half-surprised to find himself standing in the middle of the room. What now – someone coming in? Excuses and explanations, none of them approaching coherency, flashed through his mind. He looked at the door. He looked at the chair. He looked at the closet.

A soft thump on the other side of the wall indicated that someone was messing with the document holder. Hmm. What now?

The nurse pulled the paperwork out of its holder and absently shuffled through it, her mind on the television news broadcast she had just watched. Another one of those strange, sad, senseless weekday morning mysteries that shocked the city, just for a moment, and then was gone.

This is what happened: the young woman had been spotted at 4:45 PM, yesterday afternoon, on the south side of Broad Street. Sunglasses and high heels. Those were the distinctive features. And youth. She couldn't have been older than 20, 21.

Yes, the sunglasses, at least two others had noticed. Sometime in the late afternoon, maybe early evening. Yes, she had been headed in the general direction of the district.

There was a small purse, but no identification. That was the first troubling bit. The second was that no one that had encountered her actually knew who she was.

Only two individuals that spoke with her had been located. Between 5:30 and 6 she had stopped and chatted with a local club singer outside one of the district's most respected artist cafés.

I felt a little sorry, the singer said. I recognized her, I wish I could have remembered her name, but if she only knew how many people come looking for the same thing she was…maybe I should have asked her to stay – I don't know…

But in any case, the woman had moved on. Here's where things began to get fuzzy. At a quarter to six she had entered a music club and engaged the manager in conversation. No, he didn't recognize her from before. She apparently knew him somehow. No, there were a lot of people like that, always coming up and saying hi, wanting things. He was bad with names and faces. Always had been. You know, she didn't even give me her name. Sorry.

Another man, smoking outside on his restaurant's rooftop right before opening time, put her a block away at just before six, when he saw her passing a narrow, trash-filled alley. He couldn't be certain, but it LOOKED as though she had got her foot stuck – mind you, there was a lot of traffic passing through the district, and he couldn't hear a thing – she had got her foot stuck, tripped, and taken a nasty sprawling fall sideways, into those trash bags.

It's hard to say…I really can't explain, I just saw this girl and she looked out of place, somehow. I was trying to figure it out; I couldn't look away…yeah, I'm almost positive it was her. But whoever it was, she seemed to fall straight into the trash bags. Seemed to? Well, it was hard to be sure because right after that a tall truck or something drove by, blocking my view for – well, couldn't have been more than a second or two, right?

Regardless of the man's story, she was gone. Just like that. Not another sighting, not a trace until…

Oh! But the nurse didn't want to think about that. It was just sad, that's all. One sad story out of a million in the city.

Replacing the papers in their plastic holder, trying to forget about the news, she opened the door.

Energized by the interruption of his reflections, Adam suddenly felt mischievous. Why not? No matter what there'd be explaining to do – a rapid, stuttering clunker of an excuse: thought this was my kid's room, sat down, fell asleep…

Why not add one more complication? Twice he'd decided to leave the room, twice he had stalled. It would be wrong, it would be silly to allow someone else to just walk in and drag him sheepishly away. No, he thought, I'm walking out on my own terms.

He tiptoed quickly to the closet, opened the doors and slipped in as quietly as he could. Weird – it was like a standard bedroom closet. Wooden slatted doors that folded outward as you slid them apart on cheap rollers. And there was nothing in here but an old vacuum, a few empty hangers. Odd...in fact, there wasn't much of anything in the whole room. Didn't most hospital rooms have a few shelves, posters about various medical conditions you didn't want to know the slightest thing about, and a stack of magazines from three years ago? Or was he just thinking of visits to the old family doctor...

His haste had been unwarranted. A good minute had passed since the first noises, and now the nurse finally walked in. She was a nurse, he could tell, because the sound of her movements was all business. She was a she because he could see her legs and pink-trimmed white tennis shoes. The base of the crib, just up to the very bottom of the mattress, was visible through the slats.

I'm ridiculous, he thought. I have to be out of my head. What if she opens this door? Do nurses carry pepper spray? Do the police come in? This is nuts. From being so resigned, so beat-up to hiding in a closet, playing a childish game with a nurse in a hospital room with a baby that is not my baby. Are you kidding?

Her legs had disappeared, probably to the other side of the crib.

Where's mommy, she crooned. Did mommy forget all about you?

Mommy's dead, thought Adam. His jaw tightened.
The thoughts were back, the death was back. Mommy's
dead, mommy's life ended a few hours ago – cut off,
chopped off…

Whoa – there were her shoes again, not two feet
from the closet doors. What if she DID catch him? What
kind of folly would ensue? Screaming, swearing, kicking,
running – surely it would be the most intense experience
of her day – fear, surprise – and then she would remember
it later as the most unusual happening of the week, maybe
even the month. Maybe ever. It would be a story she
would tell. And such a small thing: a man in a closet for
the silliest of reasons.

But he had seen death. He had come face to face
with the sharpest facet of reality. How could this be?
She, a nurse… – she has probably seen more death than
I ever will. It's probably all just part of the job. But to
feel it? To be pierced by it? To be right there, entirely
unready, entirely unguarded, entirely open, as life becomes
non-life, as that which the mind understands only as alive
is suddenly no longer so? No, no, or else what on earth
would be the importance of a man in a closet?

Sweet dreams, she cooed, and left. He waited. No
more noises.

He opened the closet door and walked to the baby. Do they really sleep this quietly, for this long? For a moment he imagined some ominous occurrence coinciding with the cooing of Sweet dreams…

But death! Death, death…we are so small, so petty. A young woman, cut off from the world, ended forever, her whole being completely vanished. And we worry about what we will do tonight, and what is the proper thing to say, and what are the rules and how shall we break them. And all we say is Did Mommy forget you? Where is the truth, where is reality? We act as though the greater tragedy is for the young to die than the old, as if something more is lost. Yet what dies if this baby dies, if this motherless fatherless mindless memoryless baby disappears? Who is harmed? What is lost but things that have never been? Who could say what those things are, anyway? The woman in the street! he thought. She carried so much, she carried her thoughts and dreams and words and smiles and it was all destroyed. The secret joy that caused her to dance – destroyed, unshared. The eyes that had met his own – destroyed.

Men kill and are killed in silence, in obscurity. A man shoots a stranger. A mother drowns her child – is there any doubt which of these would draw greater outrage, greater condemnation? Yet the truth of what is lost…

Adam began to pace. He walked around the crib,

between the bare metal cart and the wall, between the cart and the crib. He noticed a glass thermometer on the bottom tray of the cart – the nurse must have left it, he thought – and picked it up. It was heavier than it looked, very solidly built. He moved to the window, looked out. Down below, traffic moved in rows. A few people were out on the sidewalk. The sky was blue. He glanced over his shoulder, at the clock. Nine. Time was slow...

He gazed back out the window, at the city's skyline, at the blue sky behind. The sun was warm on the right side of his cheek, and he was again struck by the old nostalgia. Oh, for the days of youth, before there were lies, before everything had to be fathomed, before everything was found lacking! Before he was found lacking...oh, but what was the purpose? He knew well what the world told you to do. He felt the overwhelming thrust of society. Society told you to go and succeed, to follow a clear path of your choosing, to get rich, to win the girl, to have the child...

The sharp bite of nostalgia came and went, supplanted by a crushing weight, the weight of pure disillusionment, squeezing his chest and sapping his strength and causing his head to droop against the glass.

Society had cast off religion, just as he had. That was surely for the better. But what was left? Was it simply a new lie, the lie of success? The lie of chasing after things and experiences and success, success, success until he suddenly found himself, without warning, sliding away on the downslope, staring behind and clutching for the things that had never been there in the first place?

Was that it? How else could the arc of one's life so drastically diverge from the standard of the medium through which it flowed? How else could one's moment of greatest clarity, greatest strength and fire and force of will so easily come at so wrong a moment? How else could one find himself anonymous and ignored at the height of inspiration only to be looked to, followed, praised much later as he languished in the private, painful mediocrity of the downslope?

I know this already, Adam thought. He gasped for air. The weight was oppressive, paralyzing. So many things to do, to see, to know; so many places to go, so much expected – no. Reality has not changed, he thought. I know this.

He had fallen into his own trap again. Running the mental wheel: asking questions for which he already knew the answer. Of course! For the lie of success was no secret, nor something that must be discovered and fretted about, like he was now doing (he grimaced). Society was not a product of the thinkers. The thinkers went deeper, beyond the grasp of society, beyond the grasp of the leaders, beyond the grasp…beyond *her* grasp. Do not most avoid reality in favor of illusion? Was it not plain? Had he not been through this before, in school, after school, as he had removed himself slowly from the shallow end of thought?

Yes, and he had always came back to the same place, for there was no other place to go. I can think. I can send my thought out, open to the wind, open to the universe, and it will register every ripple and eddy. I have seen the world, I have seen through the fabricated comforts – and no, this was not something esoteric, it was not the domain of bearded, absent-minded philosophy professors who endlessly and uselessly debated the mere naming of reality. It was plain to see, clear and simple. Simply sit still and allow the thoughts to flow down and into the cracks, and you will see. You must see.

The key to life. All that is life. Pure thought. I can think. I THINK, he repeated. I can be battered and bruised, I can gain all, I can lose all (he had lost friends, let them trickle away in his addiction to *her* – it was nothing, it was unimportant), I can be given any situation, anything at all, and I will be better off than the man to my left and the woman to my right; I will not need them, I will not need anything, because I can think! I THINK! It is the purest pleasure, the highest aim – achieved! And in the end, and on top of it all, I will surely gain a measure of success (no, something beyond this, beyond *her*, beyond now), because I will think, I will think truly and deeply as

I have thought truly and deeply, with nothing but my own words in my mouth!

The fan whispered behind him. He felt nothing. It was not working. He could not understand why it was not working. This was all he needed: this was the key, this was the key to living that he knew and had known all along. Where was the excitement? This was the truth, the one truth that could be held, and so many labored so long in pursuit of so much less! If only he could get back the elation of earlier, when he had nearly broken free – the lie had sucked him under then. Oh, but this time it would have no chance! His hold was firm, he was secure in the truth!

Nothing. Nothing at all.

Adam turned from the window, nearly lost the thermometer from his tired grasp. He did not understand. The weight was gone, of course the weight was gone. But in its place was that foul malaise. Nothing. The lie was conquered, extinguished by his own liquid thought, and there was no pleasure in it. The key was here, the key was in place, and there was no comfort in it.

He slumped back into the chair. Nothing. There was nothing, and it made no sense. He held truth (the pure and beautiful truth! he said to himself), and with it came no pleasure, and he did not understand.

He blinked hard, searching his head, searching his heart. He just couldn't get up, get underway, get on with things. He was frozen in place, and he did not know why.

He knew exactly why.

Shattered

It was growing late, and it was getting cold. He wished he had thought to bring food. He wished he had brought a blanket. He wished he had another CD. He wished he could just lie down and sleep. He wished the lights would go off.

The boy was starting to feel ragged – ragged, is that a good word? Tired and hungry and just cold enough to be uncomfortable. But this was it, there was no getting out or going back. He looked at his watch. 11:30, only 11:30…

It was misery. Misery was appropriate. From misery he had come here, and in misery he might as well sit. Misery was the fuel. He would use it for his fire. I'm so smart, he thought, sneering, as his metaphor rang true. And it doesn't matter, none of it matters…

He'd turned his CD player off. Too much of anything eventually becomes annoying. Now it was quiet, only the rumbling sound of the bus on the pavement, the squeak of the brakes when it stopped, the lonely shuffling of single passengers entering and leaving, mostly from the front section of the bus. He hadn't seen anyone in back for a long time.

Not that he could see much, scrunched up against the window. It really was a good place to be inconspicuous. Still, he was getting nervous again. Nervous, on top of everything else. This was too easy! It would be nice to have some reassurance that he was doing things right: a couple passengers here and there, passing by, ignoring him like any good city-dweller should...

He began to worry about being caught. What if someone walked by, looked at him, and decided to call the police, or even just report him to the bus driver?

He pulled his backpack out from under the seat, put it beside him, and sat up straight. Maybe he could pass for an adult. Maybe. He flipped the hood of his sweatshirt over his head, crossed his arms, and stared out the window. No one will mess with this! he told himself. Hopefully.

The boy gazed out the window for awhile. The bus was now on the highway. The highway? His stomach turned sour and queasy, he felt pressure in his throat. Why the highway? Was this a new route? What if this was a new route? What if it didn't go back? Where would he get off? What would happen to the plan!

He imagined tomorrow morning, somewhere on the wrong side of the city. What would he do? He had no idea how to get around town – only where he was supposed to get off and which direction to walk. The internet had said...ok. Ok, ok. Don't panic. Don't panic, he thought, swallowing forcefully at the lump in his throat. This was bus number 12, the same number 12 he'd been on before with Mother. It had the funny metal panel he now sat behind, it always went on the same route in the afternoon. And the city transportation site said number 12 followed the route from 7 AM to 10 PM weekdays.

Yes. Stupid, he thought (he hadn't checked the night schedule, since his target time was 8:30 AM). This is obviously just an alternate night route. Yes. Seven o'clock and the bus will be back on track. Nothing to worry about. It will all work out. Right? But he couldn't shake the new nervousness, and he couldn't swallow the lump in his throat. This was everything; things just couldn't go wrong!

The bus exited the highway, ran through a suburban area. It pulled up to a station where at least 15 people were gathered. He looked away. He didn't want to meet eyes. As the passengers entered the bus and the noise level increased, he pulled his folded arms tighter and tighter. Is someone coming back here...but no one did.

The spoken sounds of another language drifted from the front. He stared out the window again. Soon there was another stop, more people. And another. They came swarming into the rear section of the bus, passing by him. He held his breath, but no one bothered him, not a word was directed his way. The hum of voices, mostly foreign, filled the air. He chanced a look around, noticing several younger people – teenagers, even. That was comforting, and he relaxed a little. The people of the city, just like Mother said. Mind your business, they mind theirs.

You use the seat?

His heart jumped. Ah, no, no I'm not, he said hastily, pulling the backpack into his lap.

The large man sat down. No more words were exchanged. The boy felt warmer. The hunger pangs had passed. He looked at his watch. Just past midnight. This might work out after all.

The interior lights went out between stops now, as the bus rumbled down the highways. The boy closed his eyes, feeling oddly comforted by the crowd of passengers, their foreign murmuring, even the heat of the big man beside him.

Slowly the crowd began to thin out. The volume level dropped, the man left the seat beside him, and soon it was quiet again. The voices around him became fainter and fainter until there were just a few, way up front. Then the bus stopped once more and they were gone.

Minutes passed, and the boy came to a sudden realization: the bus was not moving; something was not right.

He glanced out the window. There was a bus stop, but no people. His heart began to beat faster. The interior lights were all on. He could be seen by the most casual of glances. Suddenly he heard the clomping of boots from the front, deliberate footfalls that were not the sound of any passenger. The driver? Was the driver coming? His eyes darted frantically, searching for someplace to hide, his brain screaming out NO, you can't be caught, not now!

As if by instinct, he slipped fluidly under the seat, curling up tightly around his backpack. The footfalls grew louder. Then they stopped. No, no, no, he thought, tears welling up in his eyes. For the first time all night he felt like a child, small and helpless. He had been in charge, for once he had been on his own mission, in control of his own anger. Now he would be thoroughly humiliated; his parents would be called up, collecting him with grave, sad faces. Mother, Mother, stupid Mother! He could see the face now. Pity, disappointment, everything but anger! There would be no more chances like the one he had just screwed up. Just the losers at the lunch table and Jimmy and Nick and that Katie Jones. He shouldn't have gotten on the bus. He should have done something else – walked around, hid in a dumpster, at the school, somewhere. What an idiotic plan, riding a bus all night. Oh, but he had been so close!

The thoughts flew through his head like a blast of

dynamite, lingering no longer than a second. It took no more than another second for the footfalls to resume, and just like that they were past his position and fading away toward the back of the bus, where they took a turn left and disappeared. But now there were voices, men's voices from outside that back entrance. Clutching his backpack, the boy hardly breathed. After what seemed like forever, he heard a new set of footfalls coming from the rear. They sounded different; a little lighter and quicker. Holding his breath, he tensed as they passed by. But pass by they did, and a minute later the doors closed, the lights dimmed and the bus began moving.

The boy crawled slowly out of his hiding spot, back onto the seat, where he once again slumped against the window. An exhausted sense of relief came over him, mingling with the cold and the lack of sleep and the hunger which had just come back. He suppressed a sob. Don't cry, he chided, but that only made it worse. He felt miserable, miserable and relieved at the same time and it was worse than just being plain miserable. It was like Mother had come in to his room uninvited and comforted him, just when he needed comforting. Comforting was stupid, useless. Stupid Mother…

And he began crying. He couldn't stop it, couldn't hold back any longer. He pulled the hood over his face, smashed the fabric into his eyelids, hissed angrily at himself. But he couldn't stop the tears, he couldn't stop his silent sobs.

The last images that passed through his head before he fell into scattered, uneasy sleep were those of the business man, the farmer and his wife, the mother and child, and the dopey-shades college girl. All asleep, warm in their beds. Happy.

The girl was lying on her back, staring up between buildings at a narrow strip of blue sky. Though it was rather dark, here in the shadows (with one hand she removed her dopey sunglasses. She didn't care much for them, anyway, but they always seemed to draw compliments).

Hesitantly, she sat up, peering over the mound of garbage bags through which she had just come. No one had stopped to look. Thank God, she thought. How embarrassing! She stood, put the sunglasses in her purse, glanced around, and began to tiptoe down the alley, which thankfully opened into another street – a street where she would watch her step more carefully. The sidewalks in the city – everyone complained; she should have been on guard. Oh well, no one had seen, or if they had (there were so many people in the district, even this early in the evening. Someone must have seen!) they had not bothered to stop and investigate. Was that...did that say something about the people? Hmm. Oh well.

She had driven in from the west with the sun to her back, high on the grand promise of the city. A little too high, it had turned out – but no matter. Life wasn't always magic, and she was ready to do whatever it took. She had needed a little reality to temper her ridiculous expectations anyway. Yes, that was it.

Parking in a cheap pay lot just north of Broad Street, she had walked, for the weather was fine and the open air was calling, quite a few city blocks south to get to the district. In heels, no less. But it had really felt like no distance at all – it was the sweetest, most buoyant walk she supposed she had ever had (she smiled at the romantic image). The future was right in front of her and every footfall was one step closer. She had discovered what she wanted, what she was willing to work for, and today she had come to get it.

There were two months to work with. After a summer of odd jobs, singing, and heading into the city as often as possible, classes had just restarted at her small-town university. But this time, her second year at college, things simply didn't feel right. In fact, it felt as if her life had ended. Not LITERALLY, not in a depressing, angry, suicidal way – no, she had had a lot of fun freshman year, a lot of friends, a lot of good times. All of that would be back; it wasn't like she was going to be miserable or anything. But HER life, the one she was destined for, the future – it was not there. It had stayed here, with the summer, in the city. In the city, maybe beyond the city later on. But not in a small-town university, however prestigious, however many students they sent off to graduate school.

The notion had come to her so powerfully, so distinctly, that in less than a week her mind was made up. But still, she had consulted her best friend and roommate:

I'm thinking about going to the city, she had said plainly.

Right now? But—

I'm good, right? she said. You remember the times this summer, all those bands we watched, right?

I don't know…I mean – really leaving school?

But wasn't I good enough? She said. I was as good as any of them, right, Natalie? We talked about it – you saw!

Yeah, I guess… (Oh, Natalie – a fine friend but not a very useful judge of talent)

What if I did it? Would you tell?

And that was that. Within the hour, Natalie was on board. Natalie would be given first invitation to any show, would be treated to dinner, would be invited in for shopping, anything she wanted.

With Natalie on her side, all she needed was a good cover. She went to the university's web page and unselected the little box that allowed parents to look at grades. Just for a few months. She would tell them the website had changed and she just had not gotten around to fixing the grade thing. Easy. Next, she called up her bank account online and changed the password. It was time for her to have some privacy, she had thought (this is what she would tell them). I'm sorry. We should have discussed this. I can change it back if you want!

Natalie was to be difficult to contact. Busy studying, not easily reachable on the land line. If they called Natalie's cell, she was to direct them to their daughter's own number. The girl would always have a story ready. I just got out of class, Mom; I'm just going to study some and go to bed early, Dad; no, I won't work too hard.

It was simple. Simple, but elegant.

By early the next week she was mostly packed, and the plan was set. She went to the bank and nervously handed the teller a three-thousand dollar withdrawal slip. Cash. After she got outside and began breathing again, she sneaked a quick peak. *Oh my God.* Looking away, she shoved the massive wad of bills into a white paper bag and folded it tightly over itself again and again. This packet she buried deep into the recesses of her car's glove compartment, and she had not taken a peek since. She didn't know why the large sum of money made her nervous. Maybe it was because her parents had always been money-conscious, carrying very modest amounts of cash and spending even less – no shopping sprees, no maxed-out cards. In any case, she would not have to bother with the money until the funds in her wallet ran out.

Everything else had gone according to plan and now, Thursday, she had finally made it – had embarked on the dream ride to her destiny!

By 5:15 or 5:30 she had meandered over to the district. She stood up straight, walked slowly, sensuously, smiling down the sidewalk. She looked beautiful – gorgeous, and she knew it. Long blond hair, perfect features. She was meant for this. From the corner of her eye she caught a young guy staring. Then another. Yes indeed! Now, it was either run into one of her many acquaintances, or walk inside and ask for managers – she was ready.

A singer she knew appeared at the top of a below-ground stairway and headed her way. It was a woman, mid-20s, beautiful and black with wavy, red-tinted hair, a smooth face and smoother voice. One of the district's best. They almost ran into each other before she got the nerve to speak.

Jeanette! said the girl.

Uh hi, Jeanette said. Hey! You…you the girl we called up on stage a couple weeks back? What you doin'

down here this early? Or is it the weekend yet? Am I goin'
crazy already?

(Jeanette didn't know her name, which was a little
upsetting. They had been on the same stage at least three
times, chatted after the gigs were over.)

No, no, said the girl. This time I'm here to stay…
I'm in town for good!

Oh really. Ain't you in college? What you plan-
nin' on doin' here?

(I'm going to SING! I'm here to sing, don't you
know? I got the looks, I got the style, I got the voice –
what do you THINK I'm doing here?)

But the girl stammered: Uh…I was thinking I
would – well, this is what I really want to do. To sing,
you know? I'm sure there's someplace that has open spots
(she searched the performer's face for clues). Aren't you
singing there (she pointed to the stairs), like usual? This
weekend? Do you think – like, uh, like would they have
open spots maybe before or after, or…

Girl, you gonna have to talk to the manager 'bout
that.

Cold. It was cold. She had not been expecting
such coldness, not from Jeanette, not from the woman who
lived and breathed the music, and with whom she had –
just three weeks ago! – been lost in the musical rapture that
comes only from the stage.

The girl changed the subject, somehow. Well, she wasn't entirely sure about things yet. Just got into town. Wasn't it just a gorgeous day? Nah, a semester off at college, that was all. The conversation became a little warmer. They promised to see each other soon. Jeanette walked away.

Ok, I can learn from that (she felt like she had been kicked, but – but it was a healthy pain, a constructive pain, she told herself). I was too quick about it. Just think, if I were an established singer would I really be excited about someone coming to get in on my business?

Especially if that someone is so talented and ready, she thought, allowing a mischievous half-smile to grow from the corner of her mouth. Oh, the buzz of the stage, the incredible high one got from it – with a microphone touching her lips and Jeanette's backing band grooving behind her, she had been perfectly in her element. Her voice had been loud and strong, the audience had eaten it up…

I am ready, she repeated (though it did sting a little, and the soft breeze was no longer so weightless).

Ready now for rejection, she strode down the steps. The Grotto was one of the district's most respected clubs for up-and-coming artists. More than a few now-famous singers and bands had come through here.

The door was unlocked. Inside, the familiar smell of pine and whiskey greeted her. Memories…in this room she had spent a good portion of the last two summers – it was on this stage, in the back-left corner, that she had sung her soul out with Jeanette and the band. So much music, so much movement, so much to look forward to…

But here, in the weekday mid-afternoon, The Grotto was not the place of worship she was used to. The tables and chairs were stacked, the stage lights were off, and the dark brown wood-paneled walls stared quietly from across the emptiness. Only the smell was the same.

Can I help you? A young man, probably not much older than her, had popped up from behind the bar. The tone was clear: we're not open; it would be nice if you had some kind of official business.

Which she did. Was Mr. Arrington in? She said it offhandedly, as though it were not the biggest moment of her life. (Be ready for anything! she counseled herself).

Mr. Arrington was in, in his office; take a left right back there by the stage and go past the restrooms. I'm really not supposed to…but if you know him…

Yeah, sure, she thought as she headed to the back. She was so well-dressed, gorgeous, well-mannered (be ready, be ready!)

But she was not ready. Mr. Arrington was very nice. First he asked if she had a band, or a guitar to play, or anything.

No, but…

Well here's the situation. We're all booked up for who knows how long. There's some empty slots reserved, but they go to well-established rotation acts or high-profile out-of-towners, usually. I'd maybe be able to fit you in – as long as you didn't expect to get paid right away – in the 6:30 slot, on days when we have a shorter bill – but you'd have to be all ready to go, backing band, something, and 5 songs or so. And you're saying you just sing, no guitar…

…With Jeanette. Hmm. Yes, I might remember you. (The hook-in? she wondered, prayed.) Jeanette's band is a great act. Now, that's another option you might have. If you know her, or you know another band, you could see if they might have room for another singer – these bands are always looking for singers, you know. Someone for backup, harmonies. Jeanette's singing around 10 tomorrow – in fact, she was just here. She might have some leads for you, if you'd want to stop by then.

Inert smile fixed firmly to her face, the girl said thank you and turned to go.

One more thing. Are you in school now?

No…well yes, yes, taking a few classes…

Good. That's good (he was very nice, showed real concern). Music careers are tough. There's a lot of folks that scratch around on the bottom before finally making a decent living…or giving up and finding a so-called real job. Now if you've got the talent and the personality, and

77

you may, you might have a better shot. But I'm glad to hear you're in school. I can't tell you the number of times I've seen kids skip out on college, only to be scrounging around the district, barely making the rent, years later. Breaks my heart.

So good for you, being in school. And good luck getting together with a band, or finding – did I say this before? You might try picking up guitar. That really opens things up for a solo vocalist – but what was I saying? Oh yes, you could check in to some of the clubs in the lower end. Less prestige, smaller crowds, but probably more openings, more opportunity – oh, and there's always the open mic nights in the cafés, if you'd rather sing for fun than do nothing. Anyway. Good luck and I hope things work out for you.

A simple NO would have sufficed, she thought, back out on the sidewalk. How was it that by simply being nice and helpful he had managed to make her feel so awful? I was ready for rejection, I was – but not that!

After The Grotto the girl had walked east, toward the lower end. She came first to The Black Gecko. Dumb name. No, not here, she thought, passing by. Then there was The Den, which she also skipped. Below street level, and she'd never been there. The Duck, Rockville, The Meridian…

She couldn't make the move. That manager had

cast her into doubt. Why did he have to do that? A simple no…but the problem, she thought, the problem is that I always do things without thinking ahead.

Impulsiveness was part of her nature; that's just who she was. All those times…like last school year, when Natalie was breaking up with her boyfriend and going through a dramatic bout of depression (though it really had been about time), she had decided that she and Natalie would drive – Natalie would get off the bed and they would walk outside, get in the car, and drive. And it had turned into a fantastic, lovely May day, cruising down the back country roads with the windows down and the music up and their hair whipping all around…and first year of high school – oh, this was her greatest gut decision – when she had passed by the activities sign-ups without a plan in the world, stopped, turned around, walked back to the table, and written her name under Chorus…it was her nature. It had served her well. She had never been on a stage, never sung a note in front of anyone, hardly given a second thought to it, and yet somehow something inside had demanded that she go back and sign that paper. And now…

At the moment, Now had become a little complicated. But sorting things out would have to wait, for she had lodged her heel in a crack and toppled over into a clump of trash bags. In a panic (and a clear understanding of the embarrassment such a situation might bring), she had continued with the flow, crawling wildly and then tumbling over the pile of bags, onto her back.

And now, here she was. She stopped walking down the alley and turned around again, making certain that no one had bothered to investigate her fall. No one had. Impulsiveness. Was this crazy, was this stupid? Had she finally gone too far?

No. No, she said to herself, this is day one. You were ready an hour ago, a week ago, and you're ready now. She checked her clothes and shoes. There was no apparent damage or discoloration from the fall. She checked her purse: wallet in place, with plenty of cash for a couple of days. The bad luck was surely over. Time for the good!

But what now? She didn't really want to go back to the district's main street. Not today. Maybe…yes. She needed to get to a cheap hotel, get a room, get back to her car, unpack, relax, and start afresh tomorrow. That's what she should have done to begin with, anyway. Two months! There was plenty of time.

The girl began walking again, toward the new street. Plenty of time to catch the dream…

I'm crazy.

Mentally spent, Adam had been able to switch directions, to unhitch the merry-go-round of thought and emotion that he had ridden on for the better part of two hours. He'd let go of the pressure, allowed his constricted, coiled mind to unwind.

He had mused – idly, over things easier and more familiar and less exhausting: sensory pleasures, simple things sufficient in themselves to offer the fullest depths of their enjoyment. Pure pleasures that could be understood and completely appreciated – better, even! – apart from the tangled mess of the world, apart from its maddening disconnect with reality. Pleasures whose nature could be discerned simply by THINKING, with no need to parse a web of opinions, relationships, the words of others…

Like beer – and wine, and cheese, and anything else nuanced in flavor – but beer; beer was his first choice in moments of leisure. He had had a perfect pint at the local brewpub last week. Ah yes – a freshly tapped cask-aged porter, each sip a symphony of dry smoky oak, coffee, chocolate, perhaps a touch of dark fruit. There was no need to do anything but sit and enjoy it, casually train the mind on the flavors and let them fall where they so fancied. And total appreciation of all the flavors, all the sensations, could be attained simply by experiencing more beer, by developing a mental storehouse of smells and tastes. It was a self-contained exercise. You needed nothing that anyone had ever said, nothing you had ever believed, nothing at all but a glass of beer and your own thought and memory...

Like music. All you needed to understand music was more music. All you needed to fully appreciate all music was uninhibited, liquid thought – nothing from outside, no teachers, no paper. For music existed apart from these, music was the reality. The bleeding vibrato of a violin, the aching bend of a single guitar string each held so much that could not possibly be described or written – and need not suffer such an attempt. For it could be understood, SHOULD be understood – all of it! – without ever leaving that glorious state of pure sensation. Ah, music...

And thus Adam had mused, following comfortable thought lines which he had fashioned over time. It was good to think about these things. It was wholesome, he instructed himself, even as he perceived that today the well-worn lines were not as comfortable; the pleasures somehow seemed less real. Chalky, stale flavors slipped over his tongue as he mused over beer; dull horns and distant whistles flicked in and out of his ears as he mused over music. The smell of asphalt, an approaching siren...

He had sat up, looked at the clock, and said out loud:

I'm crazy.

For here he was, at 9:55 AM; sitting in the same chair, in the same room, under the same fan, by the same sleeping baby that was not his own.

But he couldn't leave. It simply was not possible. Not like this. Not after the death and the crisis and all the mental sweat that had been wrenched from his brow. How could he walk out? How could he, after opening that can of worms and reaching in and squeezing until he felt nothing but the pain of his own fingernails digging into his palm – how could he just stand up and walk out and grab his kid and move on as if nothing had happened?

It was silly, he understood. It was silly to just sit here. At least, *she* would have thought it silly; *she* would call him crazy, staring at him with that affectionate look of exasperation, a look that betrayed her utter lack of understanding.

For what was it to be crazy? What was it to be insane, to be wrong in the head? What was so crazy about sitting in a room, pondering the meaning of everything? Were not his thoughts in line? Were they not clear?

He twitched as a tingling sensation descended slowly from the back of his skull to his tailbone. The gears had engaged, the belts began to squeak. The wheel was turning again.

What was insanity? The line was drawn so thin. The flick of a wrist, the twitch of a finger…did anyone driving down a two-lane street really consider the narrowness of the ridge on which they teetered, or the depth of the canyon below? Turn the wheel, just a few inches to the left, and you cross the thin line. From perfect, normal actions to actions that would only be described as deeply troubled. A few inches. It was incredible: look at what COULD be done. Look at what could be done, compared with what we do, what we expect; see how close they are, how very small the gap between!

Society gouges into the thin line, he thought, marking it with thick black ink over and over again in the vain attempt to make it wide, to separate the normal from the abnormal. But reality is too strong. No amount of marking, no threat, no fine, no sentence could ever lengthen the distance a finger must pull a trigger. What was insanity? What was almost insanity? What was not insanity? Were there things (there must be!) clear, distinct, and thought out that would yet be labeled insane?

A local news drama had recently played out regarding a man who had killed his terminally ill wife, frozen her body, and eaten some of the remains – medium rare, according to leaked internet transcripts, with cracked peppercorns and sea salt. In court he had stated simply that he had wanted to experience the taste of human flesh.

Naturally, all had concluded, this man was certifiably insane. Sea salt!

That was the verdict of society. What was reality? Who could really say what happens in the mind? Was the man's mind a fragile assimilation of the words and ideas and morals of others (as is so commonly the case!)? Did this assimilation simply crack under the weight of a sorrow only he could know? Was there nothing left beneath but a distortion of the little things, a dim and tunneled view of what it is to live, to relate, to eat dinner? Or...was the opposite true – did he see too clearly, think too deeply, reach a place too far beyond societal comprehension?

Could this latter be true? An exhilarating, terrifying warmth welled up in Adam's chest as he sorted it out:

My wife is dying. She is in pain. She will die. I will help her. I will kill her quickly, painlessly, in her sleep. She will not feel pain. She will not wake up in pain again. After I kill her she will be dead. She will miss nothing but a few sad and increasingly unbearable days. I will bear the entire sorrow. I will carry the weight. Is this murder?

After she is dead her body will be nothing more than an empty carcass. All she has known, all she has experienced, all her memories, all her concerns will be gone. They will be ended. She will be ended. The body will remain. The body is nothing to her, because she has ended.

The body is only what the living make of it. I am the living. I remain. She does not.

Second: I have a desire to taste human flesh. It is curiosity, a yearning to expand my knowledge of what can be experienced. Apart from the taboos of society, this is no incredible thing. Have not men always sought novel experience, new knowledge, and at any cost? Do not our cousins the chimpanzees cannibalize their own? It is not madness. I am in control of it. I understand it. It does not compel me to cause harm. It is like the simple desire for a new suit. I would not steal the suit, I would not cause harm, but if I had the means I would of course buy it without hesitance! Now, I have been presented with the means to satisfy my curiosity. Why should I deny it?

The two acts are coincidental. I have determined to end my wife's misery. I have thought clearly and distinctly and in pure compassion have determined to end my wife's misery. And now she is ended, nothing, no more in existence than before being born. Now, I will take this carcass that contains no more will or soul than that of any dead animal and use it to satisfy my curiosity. Tell me what is wrong with that. Do not tell me that I am insane. Do not give to me the words of others, run deafly through your head and out of your mouth. Think. Think deeply and clearly and tell me: what is wrong with that?

Adam's ears burned. What is wrong with that?

He looked around. What could he do? What could he do to plunge through the false front of society, of the world, and into true reality? What could he do to expose the lie? What unmistakable act of insanity could he perform in the fullness and clarity of his mind?

Suicide – they said suicide could not be carried out in a rational state of mind. No young, strong man, however troubled, could end his life unless in the grip of some sort of madness.

But he could do it. He twiddled the heavy glass thermometer between his thumb and finger, imagining it as a knife. He could do it. He could place the knife right here, right below his sternum. He would grip it with both hands, count to three, and then exhale as he contracted his biceps, pulling up and in quickly and smoothly until the blade made lethal contact with his heart.

No, he could not do that. More properly, he would not want to. In clarity of thought, he would decide that the risk of pain without death was great, something to be avoided. What about the window? He could open the window – it was four stories above the street – he could lean out and topple over, head first. The impact would be brief, the spinal cord snapped, the skull cracked. Nothing to feel. He could do that…

There was a problem. A barrier to this whole nonsense. Death. The loss of everything, the termination of all thought and memory, the end of being. Adam did not – could not! – desire death. His thinking was too full, he too clearly saw and understood the permanence of death. In clarity of thought he grasped the absolute foolishness, the ultimate consequence. And so suicide was out of the question.

Clouds passed over the sun. The panels of light on the wall beside faded away as the room was cast in shadow.

Adam looked through the window. Darker clouds in the distance. A storm? He looked at the clock. 10:10. He looked at the thermometer still clutched in his hand. 96 degrees. He looked at the fan. Still spinning. He looked at the baby.

He looked at the baby. His breath halted. His face grew warm. A cold prickling buzz washed over his feet and hands.

No. No, no, no. No no no no no. But he had found his answer, he had found exactly what he needed, that which would thrust him out of the malaise…

Why not?

It's crazy, it's unthinkable!

But he'd been through all that. Those words were the words of others; not his own. Crazy was meaningless. Unthinkable was meaningless…

Why not?

I have no desire for such a thing!

Oh, but he did. It had lit up inside of him, sharp and easily distinguished, overpowering all else and filling up every corner of his being...

Why not?

The family...

What family? Mommy's dead. Battered, splattered all over the street. No father. No one to claim it... that's not really true! Adam thought. But what if it were...

How can I justify taking life! How can I claim the right to this child's life?

But what were rights apart from society? What was there – what real and solid things were there beyond life and death? Who beyond the hollow voice of social conscience could say anything about the rightness or wrongness of it? Who could say it was not right for the woman in the street to die? Who could say it was not wrong? Did either of those statements make any difference now?

Adam trembled as the buzz worked its way inward, through his whole body. His chest was full. His head was full. He was on fire. No, he said. There's just no way...

Why not?

Clouds had passed over the sinking sun and a cooler, stiffer breeze greeted her face as the girl emerged from the alley. She headed left, toward the sun, with the wind at her back. What to do about a hotel...she studied the street. It seemed to be a sort of back end to the district, apartments on the right and small shops on the left. There were barely two open lanes between rows of parked cars on either side. Despite the second-class impression exuded by the surroundings, a lively crowd meandered down the sidewalks, popping in and out of shops, walking dogs, and generally creating an amiable atmosphere.

For all the hours she'd spent exactly one block north, she had never been back here. It didn't seem right. It was only appropriate, she decided, that she stroll down the length of the area. One never knew when an obscure shop name would come in handy – especially now that one lived here. Well, not exactly, not yet. First she would have to find some kind of cheap accommodation. Start again tomorrow after a good night's sleep...

Singing. She heard singing up ahead. A male folksinger voice, scratchy and sweet. As she approached the sound, she was able to detect a simple strummed accompaniment.

Then, as if she had turned a corner, he was there – standing back between two protruding storefronts, an audience of about ten scattered in a casual half-circle. That was nice. She hated to see street musicians without active listeners – it made her uncomfortable, self-conscious.

Thank you, thanks, he was saying. A woman threw a dollar in his guitar case and walked off.

I'll play one I wrote, if you don't mind, he continued. A bit of a lonely song. About life, the city, you know…yeah, hope you like it…just one, don't worry. Stick around for some Dylan and Beatles and such – requests too, if I know 'em of course, or if you want to teach 'em to me –

He began strumming. Triple meter, a swaying folk song that, just like the best of them, was charming and melancholic all at once.

I been down all the highways 'round
Some old Atlantic bay
I meant to find the one I loved
But there I lost my way

I walked on out t' the water line
Where dreams come in for free

I begged the sailors for some truth
And they sent me out to sea

The pure, unadorned music invaded her soul, filled her to the brim. Oh, how could she have been discouraged? How could she ever be discouraged? THIS, THIS was the true power in life; this was the reason she had come and this was what she wanted. Oh, not to stand listening on a street corner, but to feel the fullness, the completion of the music rising in her own veins, through her own voice. To sing what she believed, to share it with the audience, to have the audience share it with her as she now shared it with this singer…

It was a good song, too. The verses narrated a search (dressed up in images – she wished she could write lines like that) for love, or meaning, or truth. It started in a lonely bay, wound its way through back roads and small towns, and finally settled in the city.

She studied the singer. He was a vague twenty-something, dirty blond with stubble (cliché maybe…but just right, she thought), a narrow face, an old brown classic rock t-shirt and faded jeans. Typical, she might have said at other times. But today it was perfect. It was not her, but it was exactly what she wanted, just on a slightly different plane – authenticity, emotion, connection…

He was finishing. A jump in volume and a tremor in his delivery announced it:

Now up and down the city streets
The cold hard wind did blow
I was sure at last in misery
My love I'd never know

But I kept on through the falling snow
So hard I could not see
I heard one pluck of a guitar string
I knew it was for me

It was beautiful, authentic, true. The people clapped politely. Come on, people, she thought, and let out a whoop of approval. He nodded her way, smiling. The song had ended with the power of the music. She had known that it would end with the music. They were connected. In the love and service of music they were connected. She felt it strongly, realized right then that she needed to stay here, be here, be a part of this. An impulse, just a feeling, but she knew it was the right one.

He played more songs. They were not her songs, not really. But he was singing what he wanted and the fullness of that experience was what she wanted to share. *I've Just Seen a Face, Imagine, Too Much on My Mind* (an original, maybe? – she didn't know it but it was gorgeous), and after *I Want You* he set his guitar aside and the small crowd, sensing an intermission, dispersed. She reached into her purse. She would tip the singer now, drop a five dollar bill in the case and wait a few seconds. Then she would turn and ask him something. He would tell her to hang around and they would chat over coffee later that evening, grow together, and then it would all work out. She imagined them both on stage in The Grotto, harmonies hypnotizing the enraptured crowd…

It wasn't there. She felt again, in horror. Her wallet wasn't there. Her heart dropped like a stone, cold practicality chilled her head. No, this couldn't be. She looked around, at the ground. Onlookers were reassembling (the singer began idly strumming chords). It couldn't have fallen on the ground, anyway – she always kept it in that inner pocket. Oh, maybe she had left it in the car (she knew she hadn't). Please God, let me have left it in the car! The wallet held her driver's license, insurance, cash for the night…what was she going to do without money, without ID? Dense anxiety lodged itself in the base of her stomach. What am I doing, she thought in despair. What am I going to do?

…Looking for someone who might want to do a

duet, the singer was saying. Any ladies know *Blowin' in the Wind*?

He was looking at her. He had sensed the connection. Her heart leapt. Her stomach churned beneath, but her heart yearned for the moment. *Blowin' in the Wind?* Yes, she knew it. Yes, she'd heard a Baez-Dylan version. Yes, she could sing it.

She stepped forward. How do you want to do it, she asked, as if it didn't matter, as if she were an old pro.

He smiled knowingly. You do whatever you want, all the regular chords.

And they sang it. She took the high part, mixed up the harmonies a little, sang with all her power and conviction. As he belted louder to keep up, she flashed a smile, and as the crowd increased to fifteen, then twenty, the smile burst out into her cheeks and she could not suppress it. The glory of the music once again filled her, washed away her anxiety. Without any effort she told herself that her situation could be dealt with later, and it worked. How could anything be wrong in the world while the music played?

They sang two more songs after that, and then he announced that they'd be taking a break. The audience filed by the guitar case, dropped money, moved on. The girl stood in place. She had been ready to sing all night.

He mumbled something about being out of good duet songs. No, it was quite alright, she said. Restroom, he said, walking to one of the adjacent storefronts.

She scanned the area. The crowds were beginning to thin out, probably headed for the district proper. It was getting dark, too. She checked her phone. Nearly 8:00. It was chilly, standing alone. She felt a wave of soberness as the wallet tugged at the edge of her thoughts. But soon enough the singer was back. They exchanged names.

So where'd you come from? You've got a great voice.

She told him straight, almost. She'd taken a semester off, come to the city, was here to get into the music business, play the clubs. But it was tough, she was finding out. She'd been rejected a couple times, misplaced her wallet – it was back at the car, she was sure – but that had been so wonderful, singing with him and all…

I know what you mean, he said. When I'm playing my songs, any songs, I get lost in them. (The connection!) At that moment, to me, it's everything. When I have a bad day, when I get in an argument, when I feel like the world's going down the drain, I can pull out this guitar and make it right. I guess you could say music is my religion. You can have your church and God and prayers and stuff, but I get the same feeling from playing. Sorry, don't mean to offend, if…

No, not at all, she said. She was not offended. Her parents had taken her to church often, but she never got much out of it. Music was…well, I haven't really ever thought about it, she said, but you could probably say music is my religion too! (that wasn't really true – it didn't feel like a proper thing to say – but she said it anyway, to strengthen the connection.)

Yeah, he continued, this world is a messed-up place, you know? Gotta keep grounded somehow. Whatever it takes. For us it's music. For someone else it's art, or sports…I always say: everyone's got a need to do something special in life, if only just to keep hanging on through the craziness…

A pause.

What about you? she asked. Did he sing in other places, at other times, or…

This is about it, he said. Couple times a week. Extra fifty, hundred bucks for three or four hours – oh, this is for bringing 'em in tonight (he handed her fifteen dollars). Yeah, I make sure to play songs the older folks know, try to get some audience involvement – though I must say you were the first to actually seize the moment, if you know what I mean (she smiled reflexively). Hmm (he checked his watch)…8:05, bus should be here any moment now. Got a wife and kids to feed, you know?

He walked to the curb. She followed. A family. There went the chance for coffee, for conversation, for hope. There was so much more she wanted, so much musical fellowship to be had, so much to ask. Oh! She hadn't mentioned playing in the clubs. An instrument, harmonies – it would be perfect! A bus was coming.

So, she said, do you…did you ever play in the clubs or cafés or anything – here in the district or anywhere…?

You know, he said, I've thought about the music business in the past. I played cafés, open mics…I did some paid gigs with a band. But when you start to get deeper into it everything changes. See, when I play music it's an escape, the perfect escape. It lets me get away from everything else, just for that hour or two. When work is a drag I've got the music, right? I found out real fast that I didn't want the music to BE work. It changes the whole thing, the whole beauty of it all. You know what I mean?

Yeah…, she said. No, she thought. The connection was paling.

The bus stopped.

You sure you don't need anything else? he said. Place to stay or something?

Wife and kids, she thought. No, she said. Thanks so much, she said.

See ya 'round, he said, and got on the bus. It left.

The wallet. Instant regret. Why oh why oh why do I have to be so impulsive, so stupid? No more connection. No more chances. She'd blown it. A warm bed, too…

Distant neon lights in blue and red and green; refracting in scattered images, dancing in shapes and lines, words and splotches. Voices humming and droning and moaning, now loud, now soft, now silent; now in words, now in tones, now in watery colors. The smell of burnt rubber, stale soiled carpet, new-mown grass and gasoline; today, yesterday, the distant past. Rumbling, a guttural rumbling from below the surface, radiating up and out; rumbling in the feet, in the toes, in the spine, in the bones, through the skull. Rumbling in the stomach –

The boy jerked upright. He was hungry, so very hungry. Had he been asleep or awake? Or something in between? It was hard to tell. The images, the lights and sounds of the city had been constant. Nothing but lights and sounds and smells and rumbling. Rumbling, rumbling everywhere, with not a place to…to get away, or something (it seemed like a familiar phrase).

It was hard to think. He rubbed his eyes, which ached painfully under even the slightest pressure. His eyes were tired, his body was tired, and he had hardly an idea of anything. The plan…yes, there was a plan. It was working. It better be working, because this was an awfully cold and lonely way to spend the night. The boy felt for the anger, that constant anger and despair which had kept him company, but it was buried somewhere, under a blanket of tiredness and weariness and disorientation.

He looked at his watch. 3:35. Only 3:35. It had felt like hours and hours, a full lifetime of nighttimes. Sleeping, waking, dozing, alone, hungry – so hungry! He slid to his right, to the window, and looked out. 3:30 was so different from 11:30. Not a single person was visible beneath the silent streetlamps; the city looked barren and empty. Here and there the bright neon signs perched weirdly over vacant storefronts. Only downtown, glowing yellow off in the distance, seemed to harbor any life. The boy stared, growing sleepy again. Down a side street there was a group of teens in hooded sweatshirts, huddled together like the last bit of humanity on a desolate planet. A gang, maybe? He didn't know much about gangs.

The boy sank down into his seat, curling up against the cold. He closed his eyes. Time passed. He heard voices – a man and a woman talking in low tones, somewhere behind him. They rose and fell gently, rhythmically, over the low rumbling of the bus. The shadows cast by silent streetlamps played upon his closed eyelids. He drew his hood lower across his face. The plan, he thought. What time…and he was soundly asleep.

There was a dream. In the dream was a field of grass and a pool of mud. The field was a grayish sort of green and the mud was a blackish sort of brown, and the sky was something different: not blue, not white, not gray, but something in between. There was no one.

Then there was someone. Katie Jones was there, staring in his face, telling him how hard it was, how only the best would make it after working for hours and hours and how succeeding would take a great deal of effort; pointing to the pool she said it couldn't be done, she couldn't do it even after three years and so there was no way he could do it, there was no way such a small little weak lonely boy could do it, or anything else that she could not do.

But he could do it, and he did. He turned her around and clenched his hand on the hair of her head and thrust it deep into the mud. Now she was in the mud. The yellow Sunday dress that she wore filled up with mud. Blackish brown mud filled the stitching of her dress and her socks. He held her in the mud. She did not move.

Suddenly she was facing him again, face-up in the mud, facing him with an expression of surprise and respect and then it changed into a sneer and she said to him See, I knew you couldn't, because only I can—

And he turned her over in the mud and pushed her down and down as hard as he could. Her hair was stringy with mud; it oozed over and around the ropy bundles of hair, through the spaces between his fingers. She fought and flailed and spattered mud everywhere. Her dress was black with mud, her arms were black with mud, her shoes were black with mud. He felt a burning power, hurting Katie Jones and covering her in the deep, black mud and showing everybody what she really was and what he really was.

On the other side of the mud pool, on a high, steep bank, stood Jimmy and Nick. The pool was much bigger now and it would take a good shot to hit either one of them. Leaving one hand on Katie Jones who was still struggling, he raised the other, moving the red crosshair to Nick's head. He had done this before and was confident of the outcome and this time he pulled the trigger and Nick crumpled and fell forward down the steep bank into the mud and began sinking. Then to show off his skill he moved the crosshair to Jimmy's foot and pulled the trigger and Jimmy hopped into the air and stomped his foot before returning to the same position, and he shot again and again and the same thing happened and Jimmy said Come on, quit messing around and just kill him, but he kept shooting the foot and Jimmy kept hopping and then on the sixth shot Jimmy fell over backwards and was dead but then because of a glitch he went from being out of sight on the steep bank above the mud to being in the mud and Jimmy said See, I told ya this one worked and then Jimmy was gone.

He realized that Katie Jones had stopped struggling and he looked down and saw nothing because it was over and she had sunk deep, deep below the surface.

The pool changed and now it was small again, a light-brown pool of mud surrounded by bright green grass and a bright blue sky with wispy clouds and a yellow sun. Out of it crawled a man. The man was covered in mud. He stood on the grass beside the shrinking pool and raised his arms, and the mud on his body fell away, and he looked up at the sky to his Creator and his Creator said

Catch me if you can.

But the man began exploring the green green grass and the blue sky and forgot about his Creator. He stumbled, then walked, then ran, through the fields, through the forests, through the mountains, over the seas, until finally he had run everywhere.

Then he began to build, and he cut timber and harvested stones and began to construct tents and huts and towers and castles and cities. He built and built and as he built he learned and made rules and made societies and made sense of all that could be seen. He built and built until the whole world was covered and the whole world was full and he had become the master and there was nothing else left – but then he remembered his Creator, and the challenge of his Creator.

And he looked out over the cities, over the towers, over the farms and villages and countryside, and he saw that they were really very small things, tiny things; so he began to smash them. He smashed down everything, every town, every building, every wall, every stone, every brick, every rule, every bit of knowledge; he smashed it all down and began to build a staircase to the sky, to catch his Creator, to see his Creator. And when he had smashed everything his staircase reached beyond all that had ever been learned, all that had ever been known. And he ascended the staircase, climbing higher and higher, passing through the clouds and the stars and the universe until he reached the final step; and beyond the final step there was nothing but a mirror, a large oval mirror, and in the mirror was his Creator and he was in the mirror and his Creator was him and he was his Creator, and there was no victory and no defeat and only the truth, and so he leapt off the final step and smashed through the mirror and then he was alone, floating in silent and empty space.

Floating, thought Adam. I am floating.

For everything had come full circle and all the rules had been broken and there was nothing more to seek out and nowhere to focus the sharp lens of truth; all the hidden corners were no longer hidden, they were saturated in blue-white light and there was nothing more to prove and nothing, he thought, I got nothin', ma!

His body was warm and numb, his head was clouded. There was nothing to hold, no up, no down, no wrong, no right. Only here, only now, only a darkened room with a fan and a window and a clock and purple elephants and a baby that was not his own. He grasped, trying to right himself, but he could not find a handle. His head was so clouded, so thick and clouded. Ragged thoughts pierced through like knives. What could he grab, what could he touch, what was there that could bring him home, set him straight, make things as they usually were and ought to be. What ought they to be? he thought, spinning deeper into the clouds.

What connected him? It was not his work, no, not society, not the friends he once had, not the ambitions he had once entertained. No, had he not just been through all that? Had not the world abandoned the old lies only to construct a new falsehood, the lie that there was something, that there was some foundation on which humanity rested; a lie borne not by thought but by the crudely stitched words of others? And was not the lie of that foundation now crumbling, and had it not already crumbled and did not simple, clean thought utterly destroy it?

Of course, but was there nothing else? Was there nothing else to tether him down? *Her? Her* child? Their child? But those strands were so weak, he thought, so thin, so easy to cut.

He cut them.

Wait! Wait, he cried.

But it was too late. They would not reattach. He could not put them back together. A single instant apart had been sufficient. He was floating.

So what now? The sensory pleasures? But they were so small, so fleeting, so insignificant. They were just distractions, transient things to take the eyes off of the void.

Was there nothing, then, that he could cling to, that he could take hold of, that he could plunge his thought into and so be drawn into contact with reality – nothing that could do this for him, nothing that could set him straight save for that burning red beacon of death, save for that motherless fatherless nameless baby?

Adam clenched the thermometer in his hand. His breathing was heavy now; he felt beads of sweat erupting from his brow. His leg would not stop twitching. The baby was there, silent. Surprising himself, he leapt agilely from the chair, glided lightly to the crib. His joints did not creak. He did not feel old. He did not feel young. There was no downslope, no upslope. There was only now, only here. He stared, breathing rapidly, swaying from the intoxicating buzz of the moment.

Everything was pale and distant, everything but the baby, everything but the blood and the baby and the reality of death, the pure and incontrovertible reality of death that he had seen, that he had felt – he looked at the baby's head, began to imagine, fantasize – but no, no! his mind screamed. This cannot be! Something is missing – something MUST be missing – could he not find one other thing?

What of the deep connections of mankind, of human nature? What of those universal bonds, deeper and richer than society, than all the lies? What of that common strand of love and brotherhood? The ties that bind, that make all one; beyond and before society, beyond and before culture and race and everything that has been constructed? Did these not exist? Had he not felt such connection before?

And now he searched, grasping madly. He searched

and grasped and all he could find and all he could touch was the burning desire for blood and death, that single pure reality of death, and he realized that this indeed connected him; in him indeed was human nature in all of its glory and truth and authenticity; in him was the craving for the real, the basic essence of all things, the reality which flowed and twisted and funneled itself down into that one flaming red beacon of death. This was the truth.

He saw then what he would do: he would walk up to the baby, holding the thermometer in his right hand. He closed his eyes, imagined his motions. It was necessary to remove the baby's fuzzy blue beanie. Next, he adjusted his grip on the thermometer, so that the end opposite the bulb (it was slightly narrower) stuck out of the bottom of his fist. He put his left index finger against the baby's scalp, searching for that spot – the one he remembered reading about, where the bones of the skull had yet to come together. He found it, gave it a little press, felt the softness. He then positioned the thermometer over the spot, tip resting lightly against the skin. The tip was not sharp. He would have to be swift, smooth and powerful. He took a few deep breaths, and pushed. The elastic skin and cranial membranes gave initial resistance, but the smoothness of his stroke pushed the thermometer through with a silent pop. After it popped through, the thermometer sliced through the brain tissue as through warm butter, down through the

the ventricles and through some part of the midbrain before lodging with a semi-solid thud into the base of the skull. The baby's eyes opened, it jerked once, and then it was still. Blood began to seep around the thermometer, down the baby's scalp, onto the bright white folded sheet...

No! thought Adam, opening his eyes, coming to his senses in the middle of the room. The baby slept quietly, beanie in place.

But there was nothing now to hold him back. He was floating, floating, and there was nothing on the horizon but that one beacon, the raging lust for blood and death and destruction that bound him inextricably with all humanity, with all that was true and all that was real.

No, thought Adam, against the storm.

Sit, he instructed himself. And his legs twitched and his fingers clutched and his head buzzed and his body buzzed and his mind was clouded and his scalp was on fire, but he sat.

It was 10:00. She was nineteen, wearing heels and no jacket, and she was walking alone, wandering through streets she had never seen before. It was dark, it was cold, and she was tired. She hadn't eaten. She had no wallet. She didn't know how to find her car.

She'd tried, tried to walk back from the district in the general direction of Broad Street. But maybe she'd gone too far east or west. Maybe it took a turn or changed names and she'd somehow passed it. Everything looked different at night. For awhile, she'd played it cool, walking in and out of shops, acting like a patron. But the crowds had thinned and she'd come to a less friendly area with no shops and suddenly it was 10:00 at night and she was lost.

She really should have called...oh, but she just couldn't. She just couldn't call Natalie or Mom, because in minutes the whole story would come bleeding out and they'd both be reduced to tears and everything would end in a miserable failure (it has NOT ended, she thought to herself).

This had never happened before. She'd never been so utterly deceived, tricked by her own impulsiveness. She'd never been this disheartened. She'd never been lost.

The girl walked into a run-down corner diner. She needed to eat. She needed to ask for directions. She ordered a hamburger and fries and sat there eating without tasting, trying to work up the courage to approach the cashier for directions.

There were fifteen dollars in her pocket, courtesy of the folk singer. Enough for the food and not much more. Thank God there was still a bag of money, her money, lodged in the recesses of a glove compartment across the city! But this thought was hardly cheering. What good was far-off money when you were without direction, without identification, without anything to hold on to but five hours of utter failure?

She sat as long as she felt comfortable, fiddling with her phone, pretending to be someone, somewhere; she sat until she felt the prickling eyes of the waiter who walked back and forth and of the cashier behind the counter, staring at her, wondering, concluding…

She dropped the singer's ten dollar bill on the table and left. 10:55. Darn it – she had forgotten to ask directions. Too late. She imagined watching herself from the perspective of the cashier – there was no way she was going back in there. What is my problem? she groaned, walking away without looking back.

She headed south, back in the general direction of the district. There was no moon tonight, and clouds were moving in. It was very dark. Too dark, she thought, as particles of real fear began to trickle through her veins. Where were the friendly lights of the district? Oh, if she were that far off course…

There – up ahead was a gas station, its bright white

lights a welcome sight. She bit back her pride, took a deep breath, entered, strode to the counter and asked about Broad Street.

BrahSreet? The thickly-accented reply was accompanied by a quizzical expression.

Yes, she was serious. She waited

Ees dawn daht way, mehbay...twelve blocks, tirteen?

Thank you, she said on the way out.

Twelve or thirteen? So she was somehow further away from Broad Street than the district was – which meant she must be SOUTH of the district – which meant she must be way too far east or west, since she had somehow missed the district lights as she had walked back south, but...God, why am I so stupid? Why don't I pay attention to where I go? she lamented. How can you get lost like this – just walking?

The girl had never been observant, though. And she learned directions from landmarks – landmarks that disappeared in the dark. Why couldn't she read street signs, or count city blocks, or – or something? She supposed that trait came from her childhood. Mom had always taught her to look for the landmarks (where's the gas station? THERE it is!), and she had just carried that style of navigation through to her driving test and into traveling on her own.

Now why, she thought, why, given all that, did I decide to park so far away? The walk, of course. Just a random little afternoon walk. Just an impulse. Just for fun. She sighed. The day had started so well, and then things had gone so wrong. And in the midst of it all, an unbelievable musical experience! But the magic of that moment seemed so distant now. Maybe she would remember it later, look back and laugh. But for now it was gone, and she was cold and empty.

And in the dark. This didn't seem right. The buildings had become progressively ill-lit and worn down. No cars had passed in a long time. Maybe that storekeeper was wrong. Now what? For the first time she truly felt frightened, concerned for her own safety. Oh, if only it were light (she pulled out her phone. Midnight.)! Was there anyone to call – anyone who could actually help? No, no one she could think of. No one worth troubling.

She glanced furtively down the side streets as she passed, fearful of the dark things she could almost see, prowling in the night. A rapist, a thief, a gang of boys with knives…a dark shape by a fence moved. But it was just a trash bag in the breeze. She gasped, began breathing shallowly, imagining the worst…

But now, just ahead, there was a bus stop. It was not much, just a little plastic shelter. But it was under a streetlight and it was empty and at least the wind could not get in. As she approached, she wondered if the buses even ran at night.

Inside the shelter, she collapsed thankfully on the cold metal bench. She stretched out her legs, relief flooding through her feet and calves. It was quiet, and in the stillness a lump rose in her throat. Taking deep breaths, she struggled to suppress it.

After several minutes, a bus indeed came into view. Should she get on? They said some crazy people rode around at night...but it had to be safer than here, right?

A moot decision. The bus went by.

She sat for another half hour, the cool air worming its way into the shelter, snaking around and making her shiver. She brought her knees to her chest, clasped her arms around them. Another bus! This time she would get on. She stood up, watched it approach. It went by.

Ok. Ok, she thought. Perhaps the driver didn't see her. Perhaps this was not part of the night route. Next time I see a bus, she determined, I'm really getting on. I will... I'll step out to the curb and wave it down!

Fifteen minutes. Thirty. Where was that bus? Was it just a fluke, those two others? Forty-five. She huddled in the corner of the shelter, shivering. What if there were no more buses? Would she really sit at this stop until morning? What would she do instead? Where could she go?

But finally, it came. As soon as the lights appeared,

she was out on the sidewalk, hopping up and down, waving her arm. The bus stopped, and the driver opened the door.

Ma'am, you know (she hopped in) this isn't a stop?

How much, she asked.

He sighed. One-seventy-five. Transportation pass or exact change (he had not closed the door).

She had quarters. She knew there were quarters in her purse. She started rummaging.

Ma'am, I'm already late. (late? One-thirty in the morning? Late for what?)

There they were, in a deep-down pocket. She grabbed a handful of change and sorted out the quarters. Coins fell on the floor. The driver shifted his weight, causing the chair to squeak. She felt her face reddening… there! Seven quarters. She handed them to the driver.

The driver sniffed as he closed the door. You know where you're…

But she didn't want to hear it. She marched down the aisle, facing straight ahead, sweeping over the seats with her eyes. Someone was sleeping in a row near the front. She continued toward the rear, distancing herself from the driver. It was a long way back; this was one of those double buses with that funky accordion thing in the middle. Only just after the accordion, on the left, there was a weird, makeshift-looking metal panel stretching from floor to ceiling, obscuring a few of the seats behind it. As if somebody had messed up when sticking the two halves of the bus together. Maybe she could have some privacy if she sat behind it…

The first row behind the panel was taken so she went to the third. The driver could probably see her from here. Oh well. Who cared – better than disturbing the hooded figure dozing against the window in the panel row. She slid in and slumped against the window, exhausted in her relief. Her feet were so tired…

She woke up, disoriented. She clutched for her purse, relieved to find it still on the seat beside her. She hadn't meant to fall asleep. She glanced at her cell phone. It was 3:30 AM. Looking around, she saw that the bus was still nearly empty. Just one head visible, way up front.

She thought about the events of the day, tried to take stock. Maybe – maybe there was something to this. Maybe this was a message to head back to school, to take the safe and sure route, the route Mom and Dad would counsel (oh, if they knew!), the route that Natalie had counseled…the route that everyone, anyone would counsel. But that was just it. No one close ever thought it possible for you to be a star – you had to go do it for yourself, do exactly what she had planned on doing. What she had begun doing. And she had it! She had the talent, the look, the drive…

But maybe it wasn't meant to be. Maybe that's what this whole situation was trying to tell her. Maybe she wasn't ready. Maybe what had gone on today was all part of it, and she wasn't ready; she couldn't handled it, couldn't reason with her emotions (she remembered the singer, the wife and kids).

The girl buried her head into the seatback in front of her. She needed to rest, get a few hours of sleep, wait for the day. Then she could find the car and maybe everything would seem new again. The night was dark, hopeless, and she was doing nothing but fretting away, spinning into a mental wreck.

She sat still for awhile.

Oh, but the music! The music she had made just hours ago! The loss was stinging; it was like a part of her had been inflamed and then ripped away. She needed the music, oh how she needed it. She needed it to be the center, the platform from which she experienced life. That was the only way imaginable, the only way that felt right, that could ever feel right! Everything else was so small. Oh, how she had been drenched in it, drenched and filled to the brim…

A man sat down in the row across the aisle, rudely interrupting her reflections. Are you serious? she thought, feeling a spark of irritation. This whole bus and you have to sit there? What a creep…she stared straight ahead, unmoving, unwilling to give the man an opening, gratify him with so much as a hint of interest.

She stared ahead, chin on the seatback. Five minutes. Ten minutes. The bus stopped. The bus started. Two passengers walked by. This was a bit unsettling – he hadn't moved, hadn't made a sound. Apparently her inaction had no bearing on him. What was this guy's purpose? Unable to help it any longer, she sneaked a quick glance.

He was reading a book. Are you serious? she thought, this time directing the protest toward herself. For he was just reading a book – just a normal-looking middle-aged man with a soft face, reading a book.

She stared. He seemed strangely approachable, and she found herself desiring…conversation? With a stranger on a bus in the wee hours of the morning? Maybe it was the warm face, the grandfatherly reading glasses; maybe it was the conservative dress – sports jacket over a plain shirt and pants. Was that a Bible? She gave a small sniff of amusement. I get it, she thought. A preacher man, coming on down the aisle and trying to be friendly, sitting next to the loneliest-looking person (she had been digging her forehead into the seatback when he arrived, hadn't she?). Well, sorry, preacher, she thought, watching him turn the page. You'll have to take your religion elsewhere. It's the middle of the night and I have more important things—

He looked up at her, right into her eyes.

Hi, how are you, said the preacher.

She was caught off guard. Alright, she said reflexively. Long day…

Are you headed anywhere in particular? he asked.

What on earth is going on, here? she thought. But he seemed so open, so benign. No, she said, and told him about the wallet, and the car, and being lost. But it was alright, she said, morning would come, she had a plan in place. What about him?

He'd just come from a house call, he told her, lifting the Bible as if to clarify. A church member had just passed away, and the preacher had been called in to offer his support. There had been great sadness in the household, but joy too. The young man had been ill for a long time, and now he had gone to be with Jesus.

Mmm, the girl murmured, smiling halfheartedly. She pulled out her cell phone (it was almost four), pressed some buttons, looked busy. This awkward conversation needed to end. He looked back at his Bible.

But presently he spoke again. Ok, I'll be honest…I didn't just sit down here to make you uncomfortable, you know. (Oh, really?) He explained: for some reason, as he stepped onto the bus he seemed to have received some prodding from God himself. (Sure, sure…) And he could see that she'd had a rough time of it. Tell me, he said, what's the matter?

119

Despite herself, despite the late-night bizarreness of the situation, despite her contempt for the nonsense he represented, she was somehow absolutely comfortable in his presence, speaking to his face. She told him everything – the plan, the failure, the music, the singer, the connection, the loss – everything. I just can't imagine, she said, I can't imagine living without music, without having it right in the middle of things, without it being my work and passion – and I'm ready to do it, I can do it, but…

She rambled, let it flow like a river from her soul, releasing the deep sentiments she usually kept locked away.

Wait, he said. Music in the center?

Yes! she said. If the music was taken away her whole life would collapse, she would be miserable and empty!

I want to tell you a story, he said, leaning forward.

But – but listen, did he not hear? How could he help her, how could he hope to console her while the music was silent, absent – on a bus, in the middle of the night?

"Listen," said the preacher. "Let us speak plainly."

I am drenched in it. I am filled with it, covered in it; I smell it, breathe it. Oh, the blood – the lust for it! The truth of it! The crumbling, stumbling human race, and what feeble things we tell ourselves…where is shelter? What can give me shelter? What can draw me out, draw me away from my own dirty, filthy soul…Oh, but even now I am clutching it, clinging to it in desperation. The thrill! Motel money murder madness! Haha! Sing it out! Scream it out! Madness, madness! Am I mad? But what is madness? Who thinks truly and deeply and is not mad? What else is there? Where is a separate truth, who can give me an answer? Who can show me reality more profound than that of here and now, at this very moment? Should and should not. Why and why not. What are these?

He could not stop the torrent. His whole being burned for this moment, desired it like nothing he had ever desired. Through his head flashed his entire life, his future, everything – visions of mediocrity, success even, *her*, a son, increased wealth and standing in society, the submission of the mind and the breaking of the body, the downslope, hanging on, hanging on to *her*, hanging on to wealth, hanging on to nothing, banishing his thought, living in falsehood unto himself, speaking the words of others – no, no, no! Here was life, here was the heavy side of the scale! Everything before and beyond this was a pale weightless emptiness.

He stepped forward, sweating and burning. Suddenly his head cleared. The air became cool, and he sensed everything. The whisper of the spinning fan. The air sliding across his arms, evaporating the beads of sweat on his forehead. The ticking of the clock. The baby's breath. His own breath. His own dirty, filthy breath, black and numb as midnight fog.

Why not?

Why not?

Why not?

There was no reply. This was it. He moved to the baby. He slid the cap gently off its head. He looked at the thermometer in his right hand. Grasping it with his left hand, he readjusted the grip. Lightly, very lightly, he ran his left hand over the baby's scalp, through its soft hair, searching for the depression. He found the depression. He pushed it softly with his thumb. It gave. He looked at the blunt tip of the thermometer. He would have to be swift – powerful, smooth, and swift. He aligned the thermometer, touching the tip to the baby's skin. The flick of a wrist, the twitch of a finger! He took deep breaths. He clenched his fist. He clenched his teeth.

Adam stepped back, gasping. Had he almost murdered a baby?

"I was raised in wealth, in comfort, perhaps like you. In my forty-two years, I have never known want, need, desperation.

"And yet I too felt compelled, as you are now, to strive for something greater, something noble. For me it was charity, reaching out to those who had never known comfort or safety. And this striving was for many years the focus – the center – of my life, the avenue on which I pursued purpose, the way in which I justified myself unto the world. Through it I have seen so many things – all the shapes and colors of humanity, of the body, of the spirit.

"I have seen children born. I have seen children die. I have seen the crippled sustained by the smallest of victories, the strong and healthy paralyzed by the smallest of defeats. I have watched youth destroyed, young men cut down in the street. I have seen shootings, killings, maimings, amputations; I have looked on as some come out alive, others dead, others as living dead. I have held the dying hand of a strong man terrified by looming mortality;

a poor man rejoicing at the promise of release; a rich man as he disowns his life, disowns his soul, breaks down in the blank emptiness of his end.

"I have seen conviction evaporate. I have seen dreams evaporate. I have seen dreamers on fire, passion exploding from every pore. I have seen the fire die and the passion destroyed. I have seen the lives of the strong, the directed, the successful plunged into despair. I have seen the center ripped out of life. I have seen lifetimes of practice and skill rendered useless in an instant. I have seen athletes injured, their days of running over; musicians too – I knew a concert pianist of highest caliber who lost a hand (he looked at her as he said this). I've seen everything ripped away: sons and daughters lost and never found, wives and husbands run off and never returned, businessmen ruined in one swoop of the market; I have seen all of these lose heart, lose spirit, shrink away and not know why. I have seen them hollowed out, emptied in abject loss, grasping for something to pull them through and finding nothing.

"In my head I have known the crisis: the fragmentation of truth, the trampling down of the Great Conversation. I have felt society heave and strain, cracking up, disintegrating, smashing up against its ending point, its wall of saturation. I've seen the bare bones of the soul, the withering and drying of the soul, the pure destruction of the soul. I have lived in the midst of the storm, felt the wind blowing east and the wind blowing west, the rain and the calm, madness and peace, joy and desperation, blind hope and blind despair, and I have lived in the midst of it all and felt it so deeply and yet felt so apart, so helpless.

"For years I watched all this and thought to myself, 'How can this be improved? How can I help humanity right itself, progress forward?' – for that was my life's purpose, of course. I tortured myself with this question, night after night, year after year. Some days I felt as though I were doing a noble duty, helping humanity find itself, find its true strength; some days I felt as though it were all for nothing and my life but a terrible waste.

"At that time I leaned on nothing but myself, for I was healthy, well-off, and could admit no need of my own. But as the years went on and everything remained unchanged, the days of purpose became few, the nights of despair multiplied, and I felt myself sliding toward the same hopeless state of utter nothingness that I had for so long watched safely from above.

"I began to search – for what, I really didn't know. I went to classes. I went to seminars. I listened and watched and learned about the good in people – the fundamental good that wanted only to be released! – yet when I came back, when I walked the streets, I could not find it. I saw only what I had seen before. And my heart was in constant pain.

"It might have gone on this way. I do not know... maybe I would have done something desperate. But three years ago I entered a hotel in a distant city, checked in for a weekend leadership conference – still searching, still hoping that the revelation might come. On the nightstand in my room was a book – a Bible, and not placed there by some organization. It was somebody's Bible, well-used, worn around the edges. Yet it had no name on it. I felt the sheer coincidence of the situation and knew that despite my beliefs, despite all that I thought I knew, I would not feel right until I had obligingly opened the book and read a verse or two. It was just such a coincidence, like something from a movie – and it wouldn't be right to ignore the script.

"But of course I didn't really want to get involved. I didn't want to read one of those condemning verses that make a person feel awful about things. I was already doing enough of that. I didn't want an added burden. I wanted to open that book, read something meaningless, satisfy the moment, and be done with it. So I opened the Bible down the middle, figuring that I would not hit the gospels or anything too near them.

"I moved my eyes immediately to beginning of the page and read:

Cursed is the one who trusts in man,

who depends on flesh for his strength
and whose heart turns away from the Lord.
He will be like a bush in the wastelands;
he will not see prosperity when it comes.
He will dwell in the parched places of the desert,
in a salt land where no one lives.

"For five minutes I stared at the wall, not moving. There was no lighting, no thunder, no sudden clarity. But there was something contrary to it – 'cursed is the one who trusts in man' – something that directly challenged everything I had striven for, that set my mind spinning. Yet I attempted to put it aside, carrying on with my business at the conference.

"But the rest of the weekend clanged like a hollow warning bell – the same tired encouragement, over and over. When I returned home I was assaulted with the truth. I saw men in the wastelands, good men – good men, I had thought them! – who leaned so raggedly, so vainly on their strength alone. I saw women thirsty, wandering the desert, unable to find a drink, unable to escape. I listened to the miserable cries of prosperous men who could see not what they possessed. I reached into my own being and felt the curse of my circumstance, the ineffectiveness and utter weakness of my own will, of everything I had ever done.

"I saw that the truth of man which I had believed in and tried so hard to uncover was no truth at all; instead there was a deeper, more sinister reality, cutting far below the civilizations and the institutions and even the strongest, closest relationships.

"This reality was so frightening, so horrifying, that I could not speak of it to anyone. I could not mention it to my best friends or even my wife, for fear that I would unleash this terror upon them; or worse, that they would laugh, and blindly ignore it.

"I slept thinly and uneasily for several nights, but finally I could stand it no longer and so in desperation, in complete desperation, I went back to that Bible, right back to that same spot and to my delight I found that there was a promise!

But blessed is the man who trusts in the Lord,
whose confidence is in him.
He will be like a tree planted by the water
that sends out its roots by the stream.
It does not fear when heat comes;
its leaves are always green.
It has no worries in a year of drought
and never fails to bear fruit.

"And I read more and more and discovered the great story of humanity and redemption, and saw plainly, with my open eyes, that if this were true, that IF–THIS–WERE–TRUE it was the whole of truth, and the beginning of truth, and the end of truth. And death had been conquered, and the soul had been conquered, and there was a solid anchor and a firm foundation, and that foundation was not in death but in life!

"And I got down on my face one night, lay flat on the floor, and I let the truth come in."

The girl felt as though she had been uprooted, as though she had forgotten everything she had ever known. All of her worries, her small worries, had melted away in the strange power of the preacher's tale. She did not understand what she had heard, but she felt its hugeness, felt the need for examination, and she needed to hear more.

"What do you mean?" she said. "What is the 'promise'"?

The preacher told her the story, the one which she had heard before and would surely hear again. He spoke of the beginning, of sin, of separation, of death, of sacrifice, of the blood, of the resurrection – she was familiar with these things, had heard these words and phrases lifted up as beacons of faith, as symbols of all things good. But now, as the preacher used them, the phrases were not filled with glory, were not ends unto themselves; instead, they were mere words, mere markers stuck at various points into a single, coherent narrative that was grander, deeper, and more powerful than any symbol, any ritual of faith, any hymn that could be ever be sung.

As the story unfolded, as he continued to speak, she began to fathom the depths of this truth, of this claim to truth. "I am the way, the truth, and the life, no one comes to the Father except through me..." No one. The claim was clear. It had to be addressed. If it were not false then it had to be...

But there was so much out there, so much knowledge and thinking and believing! What one single truth could there really be? How could so many people be wrong, so few right?

"But how do you KNOW?" she blurted. "I mean, how can you choose this over all the other things..."

The preacher smiled faintly.

"What is it that you DO know?" he said, after moment. "What is it that anyone truly knows? Isn't most of what we say we know simply a matter of faith – trust in what is unseen? Trust in a meshwork of ideas and words pieced together by someone else? Beyond the sides of this bus, beyond the limits of what your own senses detect, is not everything a matter of trust?

"But here is what I am sure of: there is no greater story; there is no one who has ever made a greater claim, no one who has ever claimed for himself such truth, no one who has ever demanded so great a trust. There is no one who has ever called for such a massive, drastic choice – to be granted full power, full control or none at all."

The preacher continued, describing in detail his own choice. What would she decide? He told her of the change in his life, of becoming a pastor, of seeing his work make a real difference, of the new purpose and joy, of his hope for things eternal. There was inspiration in his tone. She began to envision her future differently, her purpose differently. She began to see her music differently. She sat as his words ran through her head, imagining.

She had one more question. "What if it's not true?"

The preacher sat back, looked up at the ceiling. He looked left, out the window. He reached down to seat beside him and picked up an old gum wrapper. He dropped the wrapper, which floated slowly to the floor. He gazed out the window again.

"Then here is your paradise."

The preacher closed his eyes. "Paradise on earth… floating in the wasteland."

He leaned back, and silence cut between them. It was now 6:30 in the morning. The deep blackness of night had been gone for some time, and she noticed that the eastern sky was turning from gray to blue.

After a few minutes the preacher sat up, checked his watch. "Broad Street, you said? I think it's the next road over. Might want to get off around here…"

She smiled in thanks. She could see the next stop up ahead. A few people were waiting in the shelter. Suddenly anxiety seized her. The wallet, the plan, the…everything! This weird, random gift of inspiring truth had been so good. But the moment was closing in. She would have to get in her car and go home, or else not go home. She saw Natalie's sympathizing face – I am so sorry (told ya so), it said.

Panicked, she turned to the preacher and stammered, "But what should – what should I do NOW?"

He smiled, knowingly. "There is only one thing. You must decide what you want at the center. Will you fill yourself with things of this earth, things that will come to an end, or will you allow yourself to be filled with the promise of life that will never pass away?

"I can give you one promise of my own, from my own experience. If you accept this gift of life, and you allow the Spirit to place itself in the center, you will no longer need the music." – she squinted, skeptical – "Yes, but if you are led in the Spirit to seek the music, if you sing under the full guidance of the living Spirit, the music will be richer, fuller, and deeper than ever before. Your foundation will be strong, your center will be filled, and your story will not be that of a lonely song but of a melody perfected, a melody sounding out joyfully into all the world!"

The bus had stopped. That had not been quite what she meant – not at all, really. But the bus had stopped, the doors had opened, and she was getting off. She stood, wincing as stiff muscles stretched and weight was transferred to her sore feet. She shuffled down the aisle, stopped and looked back.

"Thank you." she said.

"Think about it…" said the preacher.

And she was off. An alley opened directly in front of her, leading the way, hopefully, to the parking lot (the surroundings looked encouragingly familiar). As she began to walk, a deep tiredness came over her; over her face, her limbs, her shoulders…she stopped and rolled her neck. The sun had appeared on the horizon to her right, glowing coolly red-orange. It was a beautiful morning.

She continued into the alley, limping on her painful feet. The shimmering words of the preacher had begun to fade. Even now, in the stillness of the city morning, they were less real, less immediate. She knew she would have to make a decision. Would she believe the truth, the preacher's truth? Would she accept this promise of Jesus? Let the Spirit enter, enter and become the single foundation of her life? It seemed right, she felt that she knew it was right – and yet so much had come so fast. Her body was tired, her mind was tired, she could make important decisions later. There would always be another day.

Now, the important thing was to stagger forward that final block and a half, get to her car, and collapse in the driver's seat. She would go back home. Yes. She would find the car, put the key in, drive back, and perhaps sometime in the quietness of her own room she would pray that prayer, accept the gift of truth and life the preacher had described. But first, she would go back to her college and endure the short-lived embarrassment. She would begin anew. The music would fall into place. Maybe not now, maybe not as she had dreamed. But it would fall into place, and it would be better than ever. Somehow things would work out. God had given her the talent (an appropriate sentiment, she thought, in light of the preacher's words) and it would be used.

Her body was exhausted. The skin of her face was exhausted. She looked more twenty-three than nineteen. But her heart was light, her spirit was light, and now a wave of conviction spread through her bones. The soreness seeped out of her feet, and she stood taller, quickening her pace.

It was a quarter to seven in the morning, a cool, clear morning in the city, and the girl began to hum a tune as she strode purposefully, confidence restored; onward to Broad Street, onward to the day.

At 8:30, the boy stepped off the bus.

He had been awake for an hour. Most of that hour had been spent trying to rebuild the anger, the contempt, the rage which was so crucial. But it had been difficult. He was not angry. As he tried to draw on the emotions of yesterday, he was instead overwhelmed with experience, the experience of the night – the lights, the darkness, the dreams, the cold, the hunger, the constant vibration. It had been so surreal, so much more intense than he had expected. The sheer newness of what he had undergone flooded his mind, pushed away everything else.

And he had succeeded. This was perhaps the most difficult emotion to deal with, as he sat there on the bus, watching the ebb and flow of the early rush hour passengers. Pride. He had accomplished the most difficult part of the task; he had survived a driver change, sharing his seat with a stranger, prying eyes, hunger, fright…tears (no one would have to know about that). He had been strong and independent. He had put himself exactly in the position he had hoped to be in all along. Sitting on the bus, with the backpack, waiting for school.

He became frustrated, sitting and waiting for the

anger, the anger he could usually count on. He put his headphones back on. Same CD.

Let 'em know they're all to blame–

He was tired of the song. He'd heard it too much, its emotion had lost freshness. He skipped through the tracks, settling on the quietest, least aggressive song, which he had never really paid attention to (musically, it never seemed to fit with his mindset).

I stood up on the stage
And quietly did pray
That what was to be would be…
So much better!

Now sweet Melinda Brown
In the front row lookin' down
I was sorry then that I'd
Never met her…

It was sad sounding. Not only that, but it reminded him of the task. It reminded him of his task but it was sad, and that was not right, not what he needed, not helpful at all. And so the boy had turned off the CD player, checked to make sure no one was staring, and gotten off the bus.

Middle school started at nine. Had he waited another fifteen minutes the bus would have looped around and he could have gotten off nearer, but this was fine. In fact, this was better. He wanted to be early.

The boy strode purposefully down the right-hand sidewalk, and within ten minutes he was at a corner, diagonally across from the block on which the school sat. It was a large block with plenty of room for the building itself, a soccer field, several outdoor basketball courts, and one tennis court with no net. The front entrance of the school opened toward the road on which he was walking, and across the road stood the backsides of two identical abandoned red brick buildings. No one really knew what they were or had been used for (but there were plenty of rumors. People were dumb).

The boy put his head down, ignoring the crossing guard – who ignored him too, thankfully – and crossed the street, continuing until he passed the first red building. Holding his breath, he slid quickly into the small alley-like space between the two structures.

It was not allowed. Don't stand between the red

buildings, they always pleaded on the morning announcements. If you were caught, dire consequences. Detentions. Saturday school. Fines, imprisonment...it was stupid. Everybody knew it was stupid. But recently kids had actually stopped hanging out in the alley before school, and so he probably wouldn't be bothered. As long as the crossing guard had not watched him...he stood still. No yelling, no running, nothing. Good. He let his breath out.

The boy waited. The buses began arriving. Students poured in. Joking boys, giggling girls. So happy. So stupid. His chest tightened. There was Millsy and the group of football players, making fun of something. Someone, probably. Like him. The anger began rising – it was working! He stared, boring his eyes into the kids he knew, the losers, the bullies, the know-it-alls...as if on cue, there was Katie Jones herself. He imagined grinding mud into her hair, covering her with mud and forcing her to stand up, shamed in front of everyone. Katie Jones, so fake, so much less than she thought she was, so much less than she was thought to be...

He ground his teeth together. He sucked the scene in, feeding the anger. They were all so happy, so foolish. He turned his attention to the walkers. There was a group of six girls, all cramming together on the sidewalk as they whispered and tittered excitedly about something that was almost certainly of no importance. Suddenly one of the girls adopted an indignant look, yelled something, and stormed off the front. The other girls laughed.

Idiots, thought the boy. Stupid. So stupid. All the stupid things they care about and how useless those things are…

Six together or five and one, he murmured to himself, not connecting the thought to anything. Six out or five out one in? It would be important.

The first bell rang. With a sigh the boy stood, heaving the backpack across his shoulder. He crossed the street right in front of him, away from the crosswalk, ignoring the yells of a crossing guard. Funny they should notice him now. He went inside, dropped the backpack off at his locker, and went to class.

He didn't listen to a word the teacher said. He didn't talk to anyone, didn't look around, didn't worry about Suzy. Oh, Suzy. He said her name in his mind, squeezing the hate out of it. Syooou-zee. Teacher loves ya, Syouzee. Then he pictured Katie Jones again, and Nick. This was important. He needed to bathe himself in everything, get angry, get miserable. Get like usual. Six out or five out one in?

Next there was P.E. He stared at Nick from across the locker room, thinking of last Wednesday, reliving the embarrassment, the humiliation, the utter helplessness. He imagined the red crosshair. *Pop, pop.* There went the friends on either side. *Pop.* There went Nick. Soon… His heart gave a nervous leap.

The special assembly was after P.E. Some motivational speaker was coming, and much of the school, including his third-period class, was attending. This was why he had picked today. This is why it was today or never.

The boy did not go to third period. He stopped at his locker and grabbed his backpack, then went into the bathroom and entered a stall, closing the door behind. He stood, thinking of nothing, nothing except six out or five out one in. The noise of kids moving about in the hall became quieter. He looked at his watch. 10:49. He stared at the door in front of him, which was covered in scribbles. He only read one. FucK U, it said. He repeated the phrase to himself, again and again, sneering, dwelling on the F sound, building up pressure and then spitting it out. The bell rang. It was time. He needed to get there before the presentation started. He slipped out of the stall, out of the bathroom and into the hallway. A few kids, late to class, rushed by. He made his way to the auditorium. They had closed the doors. He opened one quietly, stepping into the dim light at the back of the room. The stage was empty. It had not started yet. Good. He walked to the back-right corner of the auditorium, and then down the aisle, toward the stage-right steps.

Without thinking, he held his breath. His legs grew

heavy. His fingers grew numb. His ears started ringing. He reached the stage, staggered up the steps, hardly able to raise one foot above the other, and stumbled to the middle. He set the backpack down. It would be six, or five and then one. He couldn't decide. He felt weird, very heavy. Everything seemed so slow. The room was silent. Was the audience quiet? Was the audience paying attention? He couldn't tell. It was hard to hear. He looked out over the faces. They looked back. Where would—?...in the front row, of course. Shifting his gaze he found Katie Jones.

Her face released him in a surge of rage and purpose. He began breathing again. This was it. His body felt normal, able. He had the plan, he was executing the plan. She would be first; she was the one that mattered. Then it would be five more, or four and one. He was sure he would figure it out. He reached down to the backpack with his right hand, slipped the zipper fluidly up and around. He put his left hand in, unwrapping the cloth bundle. He picked up the gun and pressed the grip against his right palm. He closed the fingers of his right hand around the grip. He pushed the safety off with his left hand, then wrapped it around his right to steady his aim. He raised the gun, aligned the sight at Katie Jones's head. There was no red crosshair. There was only the cold metal in his hands, his index finger sweating against the trigger, and her eyes, paralyzed and not comprehending. Now, go now, NOW! he screamed silently, trembling.

But he couldn't do it.

Her stare slammed into him, cut through him in all of its pathetic, sorrowful weakness. This would not work. This was not mud. This was death. Katie Jones would be DEAD. Katie Jones would be GONE. This was not payback. This was not right. This was enormous, he realized. Death was enormous. Life was enormous. Everything he had ever been through was nothing. This was everything.

The walls of hate and misery cracked violently, and the true scope of things flooded his head with sweet relief. He saw now how it really was. He saw the permanence. He saw the utter foolishness. Six or five and one. It did not matter; he did not need to decide, because he had found a new way out.

The boy stopped. He did not fire. He took his left hand off the gun, reached around and pushed the safety on, and dropped it in the backpack.

I have done right, he thought, smiling. They will all know it, that I held the power and chose to do right! Who else has been where I am now and made the right decision? Who here has ever chosen right as powerfully as I have today? Haven't I just picked life over death? I am different, things will be different now. I picked life over death!

I have done right! he screamed joyfully in his head, as the security guard tackled him to the floor.

Later, as the officers described how his life would be plunged deeper into worthlessness and misery than he had ever thought possible, and his mother stared sickeningly at him with a new, permanently damaged expression, and his father looked away, as he would do from now on, with lips pulled tight, the boy wished desperately that he had pulled the trigger. Just once.

At 11:00, the nurse left her station for the bathroom. Leaving the station unattended was against protocol, but recent staffing issues had given rise to a degree of leniency. Protocol also called for at least two personnel assigned to this ward at all times. Something had to give.

At 11:10, she returned to her station and began going through the day's paperwork.

At 11:15, Mrs. Jeanette Wilson, beautiful and black, arrived with her husband to take their baby home.

Jeanette gave her name to the nurse and the nurse gave a quick look to Jeanette, cocked an eyebrow, before returning her gaze to the paperwork on the desk. Jeanette said nothing. The nurse studied the paperwork for a minute before looking up.

Right this way, said the nurse, leading the couple

down the corridor on the right. Most of the doors were closed. The nurse stopped at the last door on the right. It too was closed, with the light off. The last door on the left was slightly ajar.

What was that look for a minute ago, when I said my name? asked Jeanette, lightly, making conversation.

Oh, said the nurse. Haha. (She grabbed the clipboard from the document holder by the right-hand door) I was just a bit surprised. See, (she grabbed the clipboard from the document holder by the left-hand door and replaced it with the one from across the hall) someone – not my shift, promise! – apparently mixed up these two clipboards. (She flashed the correct clipboard in front of them) So, see, when you said your name I was a little surprised. No big deal. Your baby's doing great. The treatment papers (she opened the right-hand door, turning on the lights) are totally separate from the forms on these clipboards. See, there she is!

And there she was. Jeanette rushed to her dark and beautiful baby girl, who had begun whimpering. She picked up the baby.

Shh, shh, Mommy's here. It's alright, she murmured. She stood there for a minute.

Is that all? said Mr. Wilson.

The nurse smiled. Yep. After you, she said.

Jeanette slowly walked out into the corridor, toward

the nurses' station, holding her daughter tenderly, speaking softly in her ear. Mr. Wilson was close behind. The nurse walked out of the room, shutting the light off behind her.

That light hadn't been on. That door hadn't been open. Or had it? she wondered, looking at the sliver of light splashing from the room across the hall. As she turned to head down the corridor she quickly glanced back through the slit of the open door, just to make sure everything was still in place.

It was. The baby lay calm and still, its bare white head resting silently on a bright crimson cloth.

"Wait!" called a voice from behind. She turned. It was the preacher.

"I just thought—" he caught his breath. "I just wanted to know if you had made a decision yet," he said.

She stood still for a few seconds, comprehending. Deciding.

"Yes," she said. She smiled. "I have."

"Then let us pray," said the preacher.

And they prayed. For the gift of life and the forgiveness of sins they prayed.

the end